HEARTS OF SILVER
A BOOMER ROMANCE

EMILIE HAMDAN

plicit Press

CHAPTER 1

IT WAS the night of their junior prom and Reggie Whitaker had been dancing with his high school sweetheart, Ana, for the entire night. They'd started dating at the beginning of the school year and had been inseparable ever since. Their love was sweet and true. They'd simply fallen head-over-heels for one another.

Reggie, with his dark brown hair and sweet blue eyes, looked deeply into Ana's; locked in an endless embrace. Each song rolled into the next, but they barely noticed anyone else in the room.

Her long blonde hair draped over her soft shoulders, woven in ringlets and enlaced with beautiful baby's breath. She smelled so good and he could barely refrain from being as close to her as he could. His heart pitter-pattered eagerly in his chest. Every moment was mesmerizing and he couldn't think of anything that would surpass this amazing moment.

He wasn't one for putting on a tux, but he wore it for Ana. He looked incredibly handsome. His rugged looks made her smile. He was an avid baseball player and his youthful physique accentuated his manliness.

Ana wore a red dress with a flowing skirt and dainty shoes.

Their generation was colorful and flamboyant.

As he marveled at her poise and beauty, he'd wished the night would never end. Yet, despite their magical moments together, he could tell that something was bothering her.

She had something to tell him, but she did not want to spoil their night. She cared for him deeply but knew that after this night, things would change for both of them.

At the end of the evening, Reggie walked Ana to her door and prepared to kiss her good-night. As he attempted to do so, the tears in her eyes alarmed him.

"Ana?" he asked. "Is something wrong?"

Her lip began to quiver and the tears began to fall.

"Was it something I said?"

"No, nothing like that. You've been the perfect gentleman tonight..."

"Then what is it?"

She shook her head in disbelief. "I care so much for you Reggie...I do..."

"I care for you, too..."

"I know. That's why this is so hard."

"Are you breaking up with me?" he asked.

"I don't want to..." she sniffed. "Oh, Reggie..."

"I'm confused."

"It's my father..." she explained. "He's gotten a new job. A great opportunity. He's been made CEO of the corporation."

"That's a good thing, isn't it?"

"It is...except..."

Reggie looked deeply into her tear-filled eyes. "He's going to be able to work here in Virginia, right?"

She shook her head no.

"Where?"

"We're moving..."

"How far?"

"San Diego."

"San Diego!" his jaw dropped. "That's clear across the country!"

"I know..." she sobbed more intensely.

Reggie was disappointed but figured they could work something out. "Well, we can always write, right?"

"Yes, but..."

"No buts, Ana, we'll make it work! You'll see."

The move had been tough on both of them, and for many years they did their best to keep in touch. They talked over the phone whenever possible and they wrote letters weekly. Yet, as they moved from high school to college, their ability to stay connected became increasingly difficult.

They had done everything possible to keep in touch and to keep their love alive. Though it never really died, it simply became harder and harder to maintain.

Reggie went to Harvard in Cambridge, Massachusetts,

and completed his degree in business law. Ana was at Stanford in California, getting her MBA.

With their hectic lifestyles, it wasn't long before 'keeping in touch' had simply fallen to the wayside.

By his second year at Harvard, Reggie had met Ruth. She was beautiful and charming, undeniably adorable. They clicked immediately.

Ana later met Carl Johnson, whom she married one month after graduation.

Neither Reggie nor Ana had intended on losing touch or having their lives to take such unexpected turns, but neither was disappointed with the lives they'd found. Acceptance was hard, but both moved on.

Before they knew it, time had marched on. Their lives moved faster and faster as the days turned into weeks, weeks into years. Years brought kids, cars, mortgages, and careers. In a blink, a quarter of a century flew by. The silver in their hair was proof of that, despite the marvels of hair coloring and anti-wrinkle cream.

No regrets, just life.

CHAPTER 2

THE ANTIQUE MANTEL clock ticked arrogantly, accompanying the sounds of the machines beeping to the rhythm of Ruth Whitaker's lifeline. After seven long, painful months of radiation and chemotherapy treatments, she had withered from a once glamorous and elegant executive down to a measly 79-pound skeleton.

She clung weakly to the warm, loving hand of her husband as she struggled to breathe. The machines were doing most of the work for her now, but she continued to focus on being strong for her family. Reginald was proud to see that his children had come to be with them in this dark hour, but he knew the time was close. Too close.

Reginald and Ruth had just celebrated twenty-seven years of marriage and the arrival of their second grandchild when Ruth was diagnosed with breast cancer. She'd gone through all the treatment, had both breasts removed, lost all her hair, and was declared to be in remission. But it was short-lived.

Only two months after they'd discharged her, cancer returned with a vengeance. This time it had consumed her pancreas and uterus. While a hysterectomy might have been successful, the pancreatic cancer was deemed terminal. The only thing to do was live what days she had left loving the life she had. The family was dedicated to making what little time she had left matter.

She visited a few places with Reginald and her children in the early phases of her sickness. She enjoyed holding her daughter's children and was elated to learn her son Robert would also be making her a grandmother, although she feared that she would never meet the child.

Knowing that she had a limited time, she wrote a bucket list and with the aid of her friends and family, she was able to embrace many joys. Then, just seven weeks ago, cancer had spread to her lungs and liver. One large massive tumorous piece of evil was engulfing the life of this wife and mother.

It pained Reginald to see her life slip away so senselessly. She would muster a smile whenever she had the strength, but each day had become more and more of a fight. Her skin was pale, yellow, and grey. Her fingernails were turning blackish blue and every breath brought her agony. The morphine was the only respite she had from the pain.

Amber, their eldest, took the responsibility of caring for her parents seriously. And while she was a mother now, too, she was not about to leave their side when they needed her most. They'd had a great family life and Amber had no reservations about spending this time on them. Ruth was thrilled to see her grandchildren. She longed to see more grandchildren, but it would not be.

Robert, their oldest son, had flown back to Pennsylvania from his big law firm in Memphis. His wife Nora stayed back, nurturing their unborn child.

The time had come to say goodbye; all she could do was

say she loved them, and the family knew her suffering would soon be over.

She squeezed Reggie's hand and painfully whispered, "Find happiness, Reggie. I want you to find happiness." She struggled with her words and gasped painfully as she gripped his hand. He raised her hand to his lips and gently kissed it tenderly.

As he held it against his lips, the hand became limp and heavy. Looking back down upon his wife's pale face, his chest tightened. Amber embraced her father, followed by Robert and William.

Ruth was gone. Powerless to do anything more, the family released into one another the sorrow and pain of a loss so tender.

CHAPTER 3

WHILE THE FAMILY hugged in grief, the memories of the past thirty years flooded Reginald's mind. The day they'd met on campus, she was carrying a tiny, black briefcase that was bursting at the seams with books. Her cute, bouncy step caught his eye. As she struggled with the case, she lost her grip, and the books and papers scattered to the floor.

"Oh, damn it!" she cussed.

Snickering for a moment — secretly, of course — Reginald loved watching the damsel as she distressed over her material. Then as a gust of wind began to carry off the papers, he leaped into action and began to assist in catching the loose material. Ruth watched his awkward bounds and empty snatches with amusement.

"You look like a drunken gazelle!" she snickered.

"Oh, gee. Thanks," he huffed.

"I'm sorry..." she said, trying not to let her snicker show. "You just looked so funny leaping to and fro like that."

Out of breath, he handed her the last of her papers and said. "Well, I was just trying to help..."

"Yes...thank you. I needed it," she admitted.

"Glad to be of service..." he said. Reginald felt nervous and awkward. His feelings for Ana hadn't disappeared so much; they simply hadn't had a chance to grow further. Now, before him stood a beautiful brunette with stunningly gorgeous brown eyes. "My God!" he exclaimed.

"What?" she replied with concern.

"Oh...it's just your eyes..." he said bashfully. "They're just the prettiest eyes I've ever seen."

"Bet you use that on all the girls, don't you?"

"Indeed I do not!" he replied firmly.

She was surprised at how confident he was in his reply. "Well then, thank you...uh...."

"Reggie," he said.

"Okay Reggie, I guess I owe you a coffee, huh?"

"Well...ah...."

"Ruth," she said, extending her hand warmly.

"Okay, Ruth," he said. He tried to appear confident and sure, but truthfully, he was scared to death. "Would you let me take you to dinner?"

"Dinner? I can't tonight..." she said.

"Oh." Reginald looked disappointed. *'Crash and burn,'* he thought to himself. *'I've made a fool out of myself!'*

"Sure, I'd love to go for dinner.....say... Saturday night?" she said with a warm smile.

"Really? Okay...great!" he was shocked but definitely thrilled. "I'll pick you up at six o'clock?"

"That sounds great!"

His mind returned to the moment at hand as he looked down at the fragmented shell of a woman he'd had to let go of. He grabbed her cold hand and gripped it in agony.

"Oh, God!" he cried. "Why did you have to leave me, Ruth? Why!?" the groan of his cry burned like coals into the hearts of his kids. They loved their mother but had been glad to see her relieved of pain. Now they would have to help their father with his pain.

"Oh, daddy!" Amber said.

Robert took charge of calling the coroner and began making the necessary plans to move his mother's body to the morgue. William began calling the friends and family who'd been awaiting this terrible call for months. But not Amber; she wouldn't leave her father's side.

Gary, Amber's husband, had taken the girls to the park down the street, but he knew what had happened when he walked up the street and saw the dead vehicle parked in the driveway. William was sitting on the porch with the golden retriever, Jessie.

"Can I leave the girls with you, Will?" Gary asked.

Will nodded. To ensure their safety during the commotion, he took them to the backyard to play in the sandbox.

Gary went inside and saw the sorrow on his wife's face. She was nurturing her father as he continued to sob desperately. Gary was without words. The coroner had been waiting to remove the body, but it had been nearly impossible to pry Reggie from his wife's side.

Amber looked to Gary for help.

"Come, Mr. Whitaker, let's go to the kitchen..." he coaxed.

"I can't leave her!"

"Dad," Robert interjected. "It's time to let her go..."

Reggie knew the day was approaching, he'd known it for months; he knew she was in pain, but somehow he'd kept the final scene distant from his thoughts. Now the reality had come and it was more than he could bear.

"Come on, Daddy," Amber said softly. "The coroner needs to take her now."

Reggie reluctantly left with his children and went into the kitchen, where he waited for them to remove her body from his home. It was the last time he'd ever see her face. Before he left the room, he bent and kissed her cold brow tenderly. "Goodbye, my love..." His lip quivered feverishly as he tried to stand strong.

With numb legs and a wounded heart, Reggie walked with his children to the kitchen where Amber fixed him a cup of tea as his mind wondered from their presence.

His eyes became fixed upon Ruth's chair as he recalled many meals around this old table. The reel of their lives together began to unfold.

CHAPTER 4

ANA HAD SPENT the morning working on a stack of paperwork that seemed to reach her ceiling. Despite the workload, she hadn't let it shake her one bit. She welcomed the energy it created.

Looking over the numerous files and pitches, she determined her priorities and contemplated the varying campaigns with vigor. The company had just signed on fifteen new clients and it was her job as the vice president of Riggers and Roe to assign them to the right agent for maximum results.

The other pile on the desk was full of proposals created by the individual agents, seeking her approval to move their campaign forward. The job was restless and demanded the best of the best. Ana was perfectly suited to the job. She'd rarely allowed stress to deter her from completing a task, but thrived zestfully with each new task.

Ana was undoubtedly good at her job and had moved up the corporate ladder with the endless applause of her superiors and clients. Being in the downtown Los Angeles area had created a clientele most only dreamed about.

Her clients repeatedly returned to her for their next campaign; her expertise was in high demand. She had a knack for pitching great ideas and making her client's products come to life, going above and beyond their expectation.

Creating a commercial or magazine advertisement had always been an easy task for her; she welcomed each challenge with finesse and intrigue.

Her assistant paged her desk with a message.

"Hi Ana," she said.

"Yes, Kat?"

"Just reminding you of your two o'clock appointment with Mr. Rolland..."

"Oh yes!" Ana replied. "Thanks for reminding me." Then she looked at the clock; it read 12:13. "Kat, thanks... I'm going to take my lunch now. I'm thinking of meeting Carl for lunch...it's our 25th anniversary this weekend, we're thinking of getting away."

"Oh, wow!" Kat exclaimed. "Twenty-five years! That's amazing!"

"Thanks."

"Okay, Ana, have a good lunch."

Ana walked the three blocks from her office to Carl's and began to primp herself as she stepped into the elevator. Eagerly, she pushed the button for the 52nd floor and prepared for an enjoyable lunch with her husband.

As the elevator door opened, she sprayed a light scent behind her ears and proceeded to open the door to his office. The large open space was empty and Ana noticed that Jenny, his secretary, was away from the desk. Her coffee was still steaming, so Ana knew she wasn't far. '*Must be on an errand*,' Ana concluded.

Carl's office door was shut and she could hear voices. '*Shoot! He's with a client*,' she thought. Ana sat for a moment and waited for Jennifer to return to announce her arrival, but after a few moments of waiting, she decided to check the appointment book for herself.

"Funny..." she said to herself aloud. "No appointments." Ana was confused, and then figured she would simply slip the door open quietly. Maybe she could simply let him know she was there.

Carefully, Ana turned the knob of the large door and creaked it open slowly. She poked her head inside the room and at first, she didn't see anything. Then she saw them. Her jaw dropped to the floor. She tried to react, but the words wouldn't come. Then suddenly, Jennifer looked up from the couch and gasped.

"Oh, shit!"

Carl stopped suddenly and looked toward the door. He jumped up from the couch and covered his package with a nearby throw cushion, while Jennifer quickly grabbed a wrap. Both were stunned.

"Ana!" he said, knowing that it would be futile to deny anything.

She wanted to scream and kill the son of a bitch, but she could scarcely believe what she had seen.

Without a word, Ana turned around and simply walked out of the office, into the elevator, and back into the street. She fled back to her office.

She walked into the building with a look of dismay on her face. Roark, one of the partners, saw her and asked her, "Ana...? Are you alright?"

She didn't reply. She hadn't even heard him. Without a word, she walked past Kat, went into her office, and shut the door.

"Kat?" Roark said, entering the office area. "Any idea what's wrong with Ana?"

"No, Mr. Simpano. She went for lunch a few minutes ago, and then just came back without explanation."

"Lunch with who?"

"Carl."

"I see," Roark now recognized the look of dismay. He'd seen it before. Knowing it would be like walking on shards of glass, Roark tried to make contact. He tapped gently upon the door. At first, there was no reply. He tried again.

"Yes?" she answered, snapping herself back to reality.

"It's me, Roark."

She straightened herself up and sat up in her chair. "Come in."

Carefully, Roark opened the door and entered the room. "Everything okay?"

"Sure, Roark," she lied. "Why wouldn't it be?"

"I don't know, Ana...perhaps it was the look of total dismay and devastation I saw as you passed me in the corridor."

"I passed you?"

"Yes, a million miles away, but yes."

The truth was beginning to set in. Tears began to well up in her eyes. Roark saw the impending meltdown and carefully shut the door behind him.

"Who was it?" he asked.

Ana looked puzzled.

"Who did you find your husband with?"

"Oh, God! How'd you know?"

"I've seen that look before."

"Oh shit, Roark, it was his fucking little tramp, whore, bitch of a secretary, Jennifer!"

"The 20-year-old?"

"Twenty-four...and yes, that's the one!" Ana sneered.

"That stupid son of a ...." She groaned as she tried to keep her composure in the workplace. "I'm just so pissed!"

"I can see that." Roark looked at the time. "Don't you have the Thompson client coming today at two?"

"Oh, fuck!"

"How about I handle it?" he suggested. "You go do what you got to do. Just don't do anything that will require bail, alright?"

"I'm not going to kill him. But I am going to nail his nuts to a train and send him packing!"

"Ouch!"

"I hate leaving the Thompsons like this. They're my best clients!"

"I'll just tell them you had a family emergency."

"The emergency will be my husband with my foot up his ass!"

Roark snickered but tried to hide it. "I'm sorry, Ana."

"No worries." she grabbed her purse and began to leave the office. "Roark...thanks."

"Don't mention it. You take a few days. We'll handle things."

"Great."

Ana began to walk out of the office when Kat stopped her. She held the phone in one hand with her other hand covering the receiver. "Ana?"

"What is it, Kat?"

"It's Mr. Johnson on the line."

"Here," she said, holding out her hand. Kat handed the phone to Ana, feeling the tension in the room. "Carl?" she said.

"Ana? Can we talk?"

"Sure we can," she said snidely. "Before or after I nail your nuts to a fencepost?"

Kat flinched as Ana slammed the phone down. "I'm sorry, Kat, but if that man calls again he's to be directed to the sewer department, okay?"

Kat nodded hesitantly and watched as Ana walked out of the office with her attitude bouncing off the walls. She looked back to look at Roark's face as he began to take over.

"Ana's taking a few days off. I'll take care of anything immediately. Otherwise, please move any available appointments to next week."

"Right away, Mr. Simpano."

CHAPTER 5

ANA WAS CRUSHED. Twenty-five years of marriage ended at the hands, or should she say clit, of a girl younger than their marriage. Despite Carl's many attempts to apologize, Ana couldn't get past the fact that he'd cheated; she later learned that the '*fling*' had been going on for several months.

Carl and Ana had met in their last year at Stanford and had enjoyed one another's company from the start. Carl was strong, independent, handsome, smart, and ambitious. While he did tend to be absentminded when it came to things like anniversaries and special occasions, he did his best to accommodate Ana's agenda.

Together they had raised four children. Emily was now married with a young son; David was still single, but busy in the military; Rachel was in her senior year of high school, and Amy-Lynn was in ninth grade. They were intimately proud of their children and grandson.

She knew that while they'd shared some great memories, in light of the affair, she couldn't trust him anymore. It broke her heart. So, instead of celebrating her 25th anniversary with Carl, she filed for divorce.

Emily was compassionate and took her mother's side. Enraged with her father's indiscretion, she gave him a piece of her mind but decided for the benefit of his grandchild she would put her feelings aside.

David, who was stationed overseas, was informed by Emily in a phone call. He was crushed but was not able to simply pick up and run home to them. He was angry, but being stationed in the hell-hole of war, he knew life was too short to hold grudges and opted to remain neutral.

Rachel and Amy-Lynn, however, took it hard. Rachel and Amy-Lynn were divided.

Rachel would have nothing to do with her mother. "Why can't you just forgive him?!" she demanded.

Amy-Lynn, on the other hand, shunned her father. Ana encouraged her to forgive him for her own sake, but it was more than she could bear. "When he betrayed you, he betrayed the family!" she insisted.

Time would heal, but for now, it was easier to begrudge.

Ana moved out right away. Rachel opted to stay with her father and Amy-Lynn chose to reside with her mom. The separation had also come between the youngest girls. It hurt Ana to see them battle over something that wasn't their fault. It wasn't something they should have been concerned with.

CHAPTER 6

AFTER A FEW MONTHS HAD PASSED, Reggie's sorrow had not relented. He missed Ruth every day. Her presence was everywhere in the house. He could still smell the fragrance of her rose garden. Amber wanted her father to come and live with her and her family, but he didn't feel it was necessary. He was heartbroken but still very independent. Besides that, he respected her life with Gary and the kids, and he did not want to be a burden. He wasn't being proud so much as he was simply holding on to the dignity he had left before the day came when he would need the care of his children.

Each day Reggie would go to his office, meet with his clients, overload himself with work to keep busy, and would return home to cook dinner — well, *reheat* a precooked meal made by Amber.

He'd given Jessie, their dog, to William. With Reggie's workload, it would have been too hard to give her the right attention. Although it was hard to see the faithful friend leave, Reggie knew she was in good hands.

In the evenings when everything was quiet, he'd sit in

his old chair and talk to his dead wife. He believed people would take him for crazy if they'd heard him, but it was his way of coping. He'd thought about having a drink now and then to chase the pain away, but being mindful of his father's addiction he chose to evade from the habit altogether.

"Well, Ruth, you should see that new grandchild of ours...he's gorgeous. Real big boy! Robert and Nora named him Jackson. Born just over nine pounds and as healthy as can be. The grand-girls are getting bigger every day and, oh yeah, William finally proposed to Faith!

"Work's been busy, but that's nothing new. Your sister calls from time to time to check on things.

"Gary got a promotion and raise. We thought at first they were going to have to move, but the company managed to make it work so that he could stay home. Amber's going to go back to school and complete her degree. You'd be so proud."

As he murmured, the tears began to fall again. He could feel her deep within and it hurt that he couldn't hold her.

"Oh God, Ruth..." he groaned, mad that he was about to cry again. "Why'd you have to go so soon? I miss you so much."

As the tears overtook him, he was interrupted by a knock at the door. Annoyed that he'd been crying, he worked quickly to wipe the pitiful look from his face.

The evening was still early, but it was nonetheless dark outside, so he flicked on the light as he opened the front door.

"Randy? What brings you by?"

Randy was his partner at work; they'd been working together for more than a decade. Randy knew how hard

Ruth's death had hit him and couldn't imagine the pain he was in, but he tried to be compassionate.

"Hey, Reg." Randy looked at Reggie's face and could see that he'd been crying. "Bad time, huh?"

"Kinda..."

"Well, the wife and I were talking..." he said.

"Want to come in?"

"Sure."

Reggie and Randy went to the living room and sat down. Randy could see that most of Ruth's things were still where she'd left them. His heart ached for his partner and friend.

"Reg," he began. "Jillian and I had a vacation just about three months ago, and while we had intended on going away again next week, we've decided to stay back here. Lucy's baby's due any day now and Jillian wants to be there to greet our first grandchild and help as much as she can. Lucy's on bed rest and, well, long story short, our vacation is being put on hold."

"I'm sorry you can't go but glad to know Lucy will have Jillian with her. Ruth was in the room when Amber gave birth to Kailey — it was the greatest joy of her life, she said."

"I know. Jillian can't wait! But that is why I've come by."

"You need me to help with something?"

"No, no, nothing like that. In fact, it's the other way around."

Reggie was confused.

"Jillian and I have already booked the room, and, well, everything's paid for. Two weeks at Shutters on the beach in Santa Monica. We want you to take the room. Take some time to get away." Randy sat quietly as he waited for Reggie's response.

"I can't take this," Reggie stammered. "I...it's your vacation..."

"Look, we talked about this, and both Jillian and I want this for you. We loved Ruth, too, and we know she'd want this for you. You need a chance to regroup and recoup."

Randy was right. He and Jillian had been great friends with Reggie and Ruth. How could he turn him down?

"I can pay for this," Reggie said, proudly.

"Now, don't go worrying about that. You can take care of meals and your own activities. But the room, spa, rental car, flight, that's all on us. Please allow us this honor, for you...and in memory of Ruth."

Reggie was touched. He was truly, truly touched. "I don't know what to say."

"Say yes." Randy's earnest sincerity struck Reggie at the core and he simply couldn't deny it. He did need a breakaway, a change of scenery. A change of pace.

"And work?"

"Forget about it. I'll handle it. Maybe I'll get that intern to help," he replied. "So, Reg, you goin'?"

"I must be crazy...but, yes," Reggie said. "I don't know how to thank you though, you and Jillian both."

"You just did my friend. You just did."

Ana's heart was still wallowing in anger and disbelief. She'd spent many restless nights pacing the floor of her new Ocean Avenue and Wilshire Boulevard apartment. She often found herself walking the beaches at dusk, just to try and find some solitude. Emily checked on her often, but Ana was proud and would not allow her pain to hinder the lives of her children.

While she worked desperately to repair the relationship she had with Rachel, she could only hope that time would heal their hearts. Rachel had always been a daddy's girl and, while she did know that cheating was an abomination, she also insisted that forgiveness meant letting the person back in.

Forgiveness. Ana had to work on that. It wasn't just the betrayal of their matrimonial bed; it was the hurt it caused her children. She hated seeing them in pain. She hated the man, and yet...she still loved him.

Love doesn't just 'switch off' because you've been hurt, but trust does.

She found her mind consumed at times with questions. Had he been cheating their whole marriage or was this a new thing? She thought back to all the nights he'd been out late and all the times he didn't have an answer to her questions. Although she didn't know if the truth would be revealed or not, she no longer wanted to be in a place where her heart could be so desperately wounded.

One morning, she'd arrived at work extra early and discovered that Roark had decided to have the carpets in the office cleaned.

"What, no notice?" she blurted.

"Sorry," he said. "Got a great deal and, well, as you can see, they need to be done. Take the day off."

"Seriously? A day off?" Ana was not a vacation-taking

kind of gal. She'd worked endlessly and never called in sick. Her last vacation had been when the whole family visited the Grand Canyon. She smiled wistfully as she remembered the journey to the bottom. Then she remembered the son of a bitch being there.

"Know what? I think I'll take it!"

But now what would she do with the rest of the day? She decided to take her Kindle to the Market Pavilion and sit down to have a soothing cup of latte. The day was warm and sunny, so she sat at one of the outdoor tables and lost herself in an eBook.

CHAPTER 7

ANA WAS DEEPLY CONCENTRATING on the graphic detail of "The Rose Killer," fixated on the harrowing suspense when she heard a man's voice order. "Do you have grilled cheese and dill pickle sandwiches?"

Ana shuddered, *'Blah... gross.'*

"No, sir," said the girl. "That is most unusual."

"I know it is. I just liked it so much as a kid, I was hoping to have one. I guess a plain tuna fish with extra pepper will be fine then..."

'Grilled cheese with pickles...tuna fish?' She'd heard this weird order before, but it was well over twenty years ago.

Ana turned her head and could see only the back of a salt-and-pepper-haired man wearing khaki shorts and a white t-shirt.

Ana figured it was just a strange coincidence and continued to read her story.

Then the gentleman walked to his table and quietly sat down with a newspaper. He sipped quietly and tapped his foot to the music playing nearby. He ate the sandwich slowly and pondered the current events.

Then Ana's cell phone began to ring.

"Hello?" she answered.

The gentleman looked up for a moment and saw the blonde-haired woman as she hovered over the phone, continuing her conversation privately. Then, as she hung up, she flung her hair slightly and began to chew on her finger nervously. Suddenly something clicked.

'Ana?' he thought. 'It can't be.' He smacked his face softly. 'You old fool...'

As Ana stood up and began to pack up her things, she glanced back, hoping she'd get a better look. When that didn't happen she proceeded to go.

Reggie watched as the lady walked away gracefully, feeling like a fool that he'd even thought of Ana after all this time. Then, he spotted a credit card sitting on the table. Quickly he jumped up, grabbed the card, and hopped over the median.

"Hold up!" he shouted. "Ma'am! Your card!"

Ana turned around quickly and for a moment they paused. Their eyes met. Thirty years had changed many things, but they still knew each other.

"Reggie?" she asked.

"Ana?" he gasped.

She nodded.

"Oh my God!" he said. "I don't believe this!"

"Me, either," she said. "Are you living here?"

"No. I'm on vacation," he said.

"I see," she replied. "Ruth here, too?"

His face changed. He didn't say a word but merely shook his head sorrowfully.

"I'm sorry, Reggie..." she said. "When did she pass?"

"Just a few months ago," he gulped.

"I really am sorry, Reg."

"Thank you. How about Carl?"

She, too, shook her head.

"I'm sorry. When did he pass?"

"He didn't. YET," she groaned.

"Oh." Reggie could sense the tension, but left it alone.

"How long are you in town?"

"Another twelve days still," he replied.

"Really?" she wanted to say more but felt awkward. It'd been such a long time and he was a recent widow. She was a recent divorcee. The timing couldn't have been worse.

Reggie wanted to get together, too, but wondered if it would be a good time or not.

"Listen, Ana," he began. "I know it's crazy, but would you like to have dinner with me tonight? Do some catching up?"

She smiled. "I'd love to."

"That's great!" he said. He began to feel more like a foolish high school kid but didn't want to pass up a dinner with an old friend.

After making plans to get together at seven o'clock that evening, Ana returned to her apartment feeling like a foolish teenage girl. This was Reggie... or was it? It's been 30 years and their lives had been busy. Full of love, family, and work. Would anything they'd shared be the same? She looked into the mirror and sighed.

"You're getting old, Ana Coxwell," she said to herself. After the divorce went through she'd wasted no time ditching Carl's last name.

Fumbling through her closet, she wondered what she should wear for the evening. She didn't want to wear anything too sexy; they were meeting as friends, right?

It had to be an outfit that would catch his attention, without appearing desperate or suggestive. Reggie and Ruth had spent 27 years together and he still loved her, Ana was sure of that. Ana knew that moving on too quickly might appear hasty and irresponsible, in light of her recent divorce. Still, she couldn't help but have a glimmer of fascination. They'd been in love. It was young and maybe a little fleeting, but it was special. It was their first love. He was her first everything! Her first kiss, her first dance, her first time making love.

She remembered that night like it was yesterday. Her mind returned to the day they'd rode out to Willowspring's Lake and sat upon the picnic blanket under the sunset. It was perfect. The weather had been promising all day. Ana remembered how her heart pounded with excitement as she anticipated losing her virginity to her high school sweetheart.

She'd made extra sure that morning to shower, wash well, and make sure her legs were soft and smooth. She wore a pretty, powder blue poodle skirt, white canvas shoes, and a ruffled white blouse.

Ana remembered every spine-tingling moment. Reggie had been inexperienced, too, but he was gentle and kind. Nothing was taken for granted. And although they were young, the moment seemed right.

She also remembered thinking it would last forever. '*Oh, the silliness of youth...*' she thought. Yet, a part of her yearned for a little more.

Ana had no regrets. She had loved Carl for all those years; they'd had four amazing kids together. She counted them as blessings. Though the marriage was over, the evidence would live on in their children and grandchildren.

Pulling her thoughts back together, Ana continued to focus on her dinner plans with Reggie.

CHAPTER 8

REGGIE ENTERED his hotel room and nearly kicked himself for leaving his suits at home. He'd come to relax. A formal evening hadn't crossed his mind at all. "I can't believe she's here!" he said, looking at himself in the mirror.

"Reggie, you're an old man now...just look at you!" He sighed. "What am I going to wear?"

It was two o'clock in the afternoon, there was still time to think of something. "Maybe I should know where to eat first," he murmured. "That's a good place to start."

He quickly called the front desk for help.

"Front desk, Janice speaking."

"Hi Janice, this is Reggie from Room 417. Can you please tell me where someone might go for a truly fine dining experience?"

"Oh that's easy, Mr. Whitaker," she said. "Melisse, of course! It's a truly amazing five-star dining establishment. It's pricy, but I've heard it's the best in Santa Monica."

"Oh, that's great," he said. "Would you have the number?"

"Certainly. I do have it here," she said as she fumbled through the directory they kept at the desk. "I got it, Mr. Whitaker, it's 818-555-7172."

"Perfect."

"Anything more I can help you with, sir?"

"Hmm...actually, yes," he said. "I guess I need to find something to wear. I came with khakis."

"Oh, right, you will need something better than that."

"Are there any men's fashion stores nearby?"

"There sure are!" she said. "You should go to the Men's Wearhouse on Wilshire. They'll suit you up perfectly!"

"Great! Thanks, Janice!"

He quickly made the arrangements for a table at Melisse and then drove over to the Men's Wearhouse for a new suit.

As he stood in front of the full-length mirrors, his cell phone rang. It was Ana.

"Hello," he answered.

"Hi, Reggie. This is going to sound funny, but I haven't got a clue what to wear," she said.

"Formal is good," he replied. "Ever heard of Melisse?"

"Melisse!" she exclaimed. "Damn right I have!"

"Great, because that's where I'm taking you."

"Alright. See you at seven."

As she hung up his heart began to pound and his hands began to feel clammy.

"I must be nuts!" he said softly, but loud enough that the tailor could hear.

"Sir?" he asked.

"I feel like a foolish boy."

"Ah, I see," he said. "We get that a lot."

"No, it's different, I'm sure. You see, my wife died just a few months ago. I came out here to clear my head. And wouldn't you know it? I run into my high school sweetheart!"

"I see!" smiled the tailor. "No wonder you want to look perfect!"

"I feel like I'm betraying my wife, though..."

"You were happy with your wife, yes?"

"Very! We had three amazing kids, we now have three grandkids. We were happily married for 27 years before she got sick..."

"And would your wife want you to be happy?"

"She insisted on it...but...."

"Sir, it's just dinner. Let fate take care of the rest."

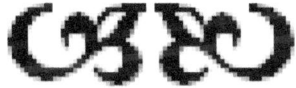

Reggie arrived at the entrance of Ana's apartment and then set the GPS to Melisse. Then, he went to the door and buzzed her apartment.

I'll be right down!" she declared. "Well, Chester, how do I look?" she asked, posing the large Maine Coon cat lounging on the bed.

He replied with a yawn.

"Oh gee, thanks, Chester. Wish me luck!"

She grabbed her clutch and then carefully made her way to the front door, ensuring the door was securely locked behind her.

As she approached the door, she noticed that his back

was turned slightly towards the beachfront. Dusk was setting and it was beautiful. She could tell he was impressed. Quietly, she opened the door and stepped outside.

"Beautiful, isn't it?" she said as she gazed at the sunset.

He turned around immediately and could scarcely believe his eyes. She looked beautiful. Her blonde hair — yes it was bottle blonde to cover the greys — was pulled up into a French roll, with a few tufts flowing down in tiny curls. Her bright blue eyes were as captivating as ever. She had a beautiful elegant red dress on and was wearing a pair of matching shoes. He could barely stand it.

"You look amazing!" he said.

She blushed a little and felt giddy inside. "Thanks." She fidgeted a little as she continued the conversation. "You look pretty spectacular yourself."

"What, this old thing?" he smiled.

Then she began to giggle.

"What's so funny?"

"Your 'old thing' suit still has a tag on it," she said as she grabbed hold of the plastic piece.

"Oh, damn it!" he cussed.

"No worries," she said. "I got it." She pulled a tiny nail clipper from her clutch and carefully snipped it away. "There...that ought to do it."

He looked embarrassed and awkward.

"Reggie? Are you alright?" she asked.

"I feel like a fool," he said.

"Because of the tag?" she asked.

"A little."

"Never mind that," she said. "Happens to me more often than I care to admit!"

"Honest?"
"Honest!"

CHAPTER 9

AFTER A SHORT DRIVE, Ana and Reggie arrived at Melisse and were immediately taken to a beautiful table by the fireplace. The atmosphere was first class, yet relaxed. Graceful music set the mood as the host presented them with their menus and announced the specials.

Ana began to skim through the menu. She'd eaten fine dining before, but this was the crème de la crème.

They hadn't said much on the drive to the restaurant; both were awkwardly reliving their memories and wondering why fate had brought them together tonight.

"So..." Reggie opened the conversation warmly to break the ice. "Without sounding too cliché, what have you been up to for the last three decades?"

"Three decades," she rolled her eyes slightly. "I don't feel old enough to say 'three decades.'"

"Nor do you look it. Time's been good to you Ana."

She smiled warmly. "Thanks. You, too, Reggie." She took a sip of water to relieve the patch of nervous dryness in her throat. "Okay. So here's the PowerPoint version of the past thirty years."

Before she could get started the waiter arrived at the table. "Good evening folks. My name is Antonio and I will be your waiter this evening. Anything you need, just ask," he smiled. "Shall I start you off with some wine?"

"Hmm..." said Reggie. "Yes, I like red. Ana?"

"Same," she replied.

"Great," said Antonio. "I will grab our best if you like."

"Yes, that would be fine."

"Celebrating a special evening?" he asked.

"Celebrating history," Reggie said.

"Oh, yes," Ana agreed. "History was my best subject!" She winked playfully. The waiter was a little confused, but he left the matter between the two of them and went to grab the wine. "Do you remember that?" she asked.

"What's that?"

"The 'history' report?"

Reggie had been sipping some water when she asked; he nearly choked. "Goodness, do I!?" he replied. "I didn't think we'd ever get through that report!"

"Remember how Mr. Applebaum tried to pair you with Debbie and me with...oh, what was his name?"

"Oh, right. Started with a D, I think."

"Doug?"

"Not sure."

"Anyways." The name was right on the tip of her tongue and it was driving her crazy that she couldn't remember. "Dmitri!"

"Oh, yes! Dmitri!" he cackled. "Gosh, he was the most socially awkward boy in the school!"

"For sure. I wonder whatever became of him?"

"Probably a successful physicist or something. He was always on a date with a beaker."

"Or microscope."

They both laughed.

The waiter returned and took their order – caviar, truffle risotto, liberty duck breast. The dinner was first class, but neither Ruth nor Reggie cared as much about the food they'd ordered; it was the company.

"So, can you tell me now?"

She'd almost forgotten. "Oh, right. You wanted a history recap, right?"

Reggie nodded.

"Okay. Married 25 years ago, but that just ended. Not good. But I can't complain. We had a good run of it. We had four kids. Emily is 23 and gave me a grandson last fall. David's 21, he's enlisted in the Marines, somewhere in Afghanistan. Rachel, she's in her senior year of high school. And Amy-Lynn just started high school this year. All doing well. Rachel's still not talking to me, but I know she'll come around."

"Not talking to you?"

"Mad that I left Carl."

"I see," Reggie looked concerned, but he didn't want to open that can of worms. "Work?"

"Okay. I graduated from Stanford and began a career at Riggers and Roe." She smiled wistfully for a moment as she recalled her internship. "Gosh, seems like a million years ago."

"What do you do there?"

"I'm the VP of advertising."

"Wow, a VP! Good for you!"

"Thanks," she said as she took a sip of the fine wine. "Your turn."

"Oh, alright. Ruth and I married just over 27 years ago. We have three kids; Amber's our oldest. She has two little girls, Kailey and Tiffany. Robert just gave us our first grandson. And William just got engaged to a lovely girl named Faith."

"I'm sorry about Ruth," Ana said empathetically.

"I miss her desperately. It was hard to see her suffering, though. Seven months of torture." A tear welled up in his eye. He shook his head. "Letting her go was the hardest thing I ever did, next to watching you move away."

"I'm glad you found love, Reggie."

"I did. Ruth was a truly beautiful woman."

Ana could see that the wounds were still fresh and she was not about to pour vinegar on them by asking unnecessary questions.

CHAPTER 10

AFTER A DELICIOUS DINNER, Ana and Reggie parked the car near Ana's apartment and took a walk along the beach, enjoying the refreshing ocean breeze.

"This is nice," Reggie said. "You ever get bored of it?"

"Never!" she replied. "I've seen hundreds of sunsets and they still take my breath away. Then again, I guess I've taken many for granted. Life gets busy."

"I know what that's like," he said.

They strolled along the beach, kicked some of the pebbles, and reminisced over their youth and three decades of history. They talked about the good, the bad, and the ugly. Reggie had buried both of his parents and Ana's father had passed on around the same time that her mother was diagnosed with Alzheimer's.

The evening ended with Reggie walking Ana back to her place. She wanted desperately to invite him upstairs but awkwardly avoided it.

"I had a lovely time," she said.

"I did, too."

"Well."

"Goodnight," he said.

She was disappointed. Was it over? Was that it?

He began to walk back to the car, but paused and turned back to say, "Are you free tomorrow?"

She smiled. She wanted to be. "I do work," she sighed.

"Oh."

"But I could get off early, and then we'd have the weekend, too." She bit her lip nervously. "That is if you'd like to hang out a bit longer? I could show you the sites."

"I'd like that," he said.

"Dinner?"

"Sure, where would you like to go?"

"If you're okay with it, I'll cook."

"That would be nice." He did think a home-cooked meal would be nice. Since Ruth's death, he'd been living on casseroles and frozen dinners, pizza, and chips. Not a great diet.

"Alright, come by about eight. Oh, keep it casual. Keep the price tags in the store, okay?" Her whit and smile warmed his heart.

"Sounds good."

Reggie waited for Ana to enter her building and then proceeded back to his car, Ana quickly entered her apartment and snuck a peek out the window to watch him drive away.

"What are you looking at?" Amy-Lynn was still awake, perhaps waiting for her mother to return. Ana hadn't told her about the date.

The sound of her daughter's voice startled Ana. "Amy-Lynn! You scared me."

"Sorry, Mom. But you know I live here, right?"

"Of course." The look on Ana's face was concerning to Amy-Lynn.

"Why do you look like you just got caught with your hand in the cookie jar?"

"Well...I..."

"And why are you dressed up like that?"

"I went to dinner, Amy-Lynn."

"Was it a date?"

"No, it was an old friend."

"You're dressed pretty fancily to be out with a friend."

"Don't give me a lecture, dear. I'm the mom, remember?"

"I know," she replied. "But for the record, I think he's handsome." Amy-Lynn smiled as she scooped up Chester and walked down the hall.

"Wait a minute," Ana said. "Were you spying on me?"

"Hmm...maybe a little."

Ana didn't know what to say.

"I'm okay with you dating, Mom. Honest."

"You're a good kid, Amy-Lynn," she said.

"I know." She winked playfully as she continued down the hall. "Well, I'm off to bed. See you in the morning."

"Goodnight, Amy-Lynn."

CHAPTER 11

REGGIE RETURNED to his hotel room and began to mull over the evening's events. Had he been wrong to enjoy himself? Why did he feel guilty? He wasn't cheating; he was moving on, right?

He changed into his nightwear, grabbed a cocktail from the tiny fridge, and then went to sit out on the balcony. He sat for hours, listening to the waves as they rolled up on the beach. The thoughts running through his head were numerous, some painful, some joyous; a million questions accompanied them.

'No harm 'being friends' right?' he contemplated.

He'd thought about calling Randy — maybe he'd have some advice — but it was late; nearly midnight in Santa Monica, going on three a.m. in Pennsylvania.

As he thought about it longer, his mind returned to their prom night. He'd been so in love with Ana. He loved Ruth without question but often found himself thinking of Ana. Every April 27th, for over thirty years, he'd remember her.

He couldn't help but wonder if his children would be angry. He wouldn't have betrayed Ruth for anything. Not that the opportunity hadn't presented itself. He was a fine-looking man; the salt and pepper in his hair only made him more distinguished.

Nothing, however, would replace what he'd had at home.

Ana's sleep was intermittent. She'd had a good time, but she worried Reggie's fragile state would make him vulnerable. She still cared for him. She always had. Yet, Ana wondered if there was anything left to build on. Thirty years was a long time. So many things had happened to both of them.

Chester did little to comfort her. The time was flying by faster than she'd hoped. She'd toss and turn, but sleep was hard to come by.

"You crazy girl!" she said. "You've got meetings tomor-row, and you're letting that foolish 16-year-old girl dictate your emotions?"

Morning came too early; both Ana and Reggie had had restless sleep. Despite her fatigue, Ana pushed herself out of the bed and wearily fumbled through her routine, and headed for work.

Walking into the office, Kat eyed her boss up and down and curiously inquired, "You look tired. Did you not enjoy your day off?"

"On the contrary, Kat. It was a fabulous day. Just a very sleepless night."

"I see." Kat didn't inquire further as it wasn't her place, but she was curious.

"Can I confide in you?" Ana asked.

"Sure you can," Kat replied. "I've been working for you for over eight years. You can trust me."

"I know. You've always been a faithful employee, but this is...personal."

"I'm listening."

"Come inside?" Ana gestured for Kat to join her in the office where they could talk privately.

Kat shut the door and turned her attention to Ana.

"So, yesterday I went down to the Pavilion and was reading my eBook when I heard someone order a strange concoction. I've only ever known one person known who'd order something like that. I'm sure there are others, but it caught my attention. At first, I told myself it was just a strange coincidence. But when I left the restaurant, I forgot my credit card, and this man, well, he saw the card and ran after me. It took a moment for us to recognize one another."

She paused and Kat was eager to know the rest. "What happened?" she asked.

"It was Reggie Whitaker, my high school boyfriend."

"Oh?"

"We were dating when I lived in Pennsylvania. We

were crazy about one another. In fact, he was my first...you know."

Kat understood.

"Anyways, we eventually moved on with our lives, but there was never really any closure. It was simply impossible to keep in touch. We wrote and called as much as possible, but it just got so crazy once we began college."

"And now?"

"Well, he's here on vacation. But..."

"But what?"

"He's just getting over the loss of his wife. He's still hurting."

"I see. But that's not to say that in time he can't love again, right?"

"I know."

"Ana, if I may?"

Ana nodded.

"Just go with the flow. Whatever will be, will be."

Ana knew she was right. They'd been in love before. Maybe people do get second chances. At least she hoped in this case they would.

CHAPTER 12

IT HAD BEEN A LONG DAY. Ana completed her workload for the day, and now it was time to see if second chances existed.

Walking into the house, she saw Amy-Lynn sitting upon the sectional, watching a Hannah Montana rerun.

"Hi, Mom," she said.

"Hey, sweetie," Ana said. "I thought you were going to Julia's?"

"She's got the flu, why?"

"No problem, just wondered if you'd be okay with having dinner with my old friend tonight."

"Who? That guy?"

"Yes."

"Sure, Mom, I'm cool with it."

"Great. Can you help me tidy up a bit?"

"Marcy cleaned already today. The place is spotless," Amy-Lynn replied.

"I know. I just want to straighten up the magazines and things."

"Wow! This friend must be pretty special."

Ana acknowledged her comment with a simple smile but refrained from revealing her anxiousness.

"Well, Mom," said Amy-Lynn, "If you're going to make this fellow interested, you need to get freshened up!"

"I beg your pardon?"

"You look too...business-y."

With the help of Amy-Lynn, Ana found her most 'suitable' casual outfit and prepared a delicious meal of southern fried chicken, mashed potatoes, gravy, green beans, and apple pie. If she remembered right, those were his favorites when he was a teenager.

They heard the buzz of the intercom.

"Do you want me to get it?" asked Amy-Lynn.

"Yes, please."

"Hi there," Amy-Lynn said through the intercom. "Come on up!"

"Thank you," he replied as he pulled the released door open.

Amy-Lynn was eager to 'snoop' and kept her eye on the peephole to watch him walk from the elevator to their door. She paused for a moment while she waited for him to knock. After his three quick taps on the door, she paused only long enough for him to be 'unaware' of her snoopiness.

Opening the door, she smiled. "Come in, Mr. Whitaker," she said.

"Well, hi there. Amy-Lynn, right?"

"Yes, that's right."

"You're the spitting image of your mother," he said.

"Yeah, I get that a lot." The blonde-haired, blue-eyed girl gallantly bounced down the hallway announcing, "Be right back!"

He snickered and was immediately impressed by the young lady. As he kicked off his shoes and made his way to the sectional sofa, he could hear the conversation down the hall.

"He's here, Mom," Amy-Lynn announced. "Handsome, too."

Reggie giggled again. He couldn't hear Ana's side of the conversation, but he envisioned her being embarrassed by the remark.

As he waited, a large black and white cat leaped onto the sofa and meowed in his face.

"Gracious!" he gasped. "Big cat! Wow!" He carefully patted the cat on the head in greeting. He tried to stop petting it, but the cat insisted he continues.

"Oh, I'm sorry," Ana said as she entered the room. "Chester can be a bit over-friendly."

"It's alright." Reggie took a good look at her as she moved to the living room area and sat in a chair to the left.

"You look nice, Ana."

"Thanks. You, too."

Chester continued to insist on Reggie's affections. "Big cat!" he said.

"He's a Maine Coon. They're a big breed."

"I can see that."

"Mom, dinner's ready!" Amy-Lynn chimed from the kitchen.

"Alright, dear."

"She's charming," Reggie said.

"Thanks."

"Reminds me of you."

"I get that a lot."

Reggie laughed. "That's what she said."

"You're not allergic, are you?"

"No. I like animals. We had a dog. A golden retriever named Jessie. She was four. I gave her to William. I don't have time to care for her. Ruth did all that." It was the first time he'd been able to talk about her since she died without tearing up.

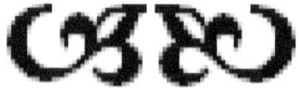

The three of them sat down at the elegantly set table. Amy-Lynn had snuck to the corner and picked up three yellow daffodils to place in the middle of the table. Ana was surprised to see them there.

"Did you get the flowers, Amy-Lynn?" Her daughter nodded. "Thanks, sweetheart, they're lovely."

Amy-Lynn smiled.

"Fried chicken? Mashed potatoes? Gravy?" He was impressed. "You remembered."

"Every bit," Ana said.

"She even baked an apple pie!" Amy-Lynn said.

Reggie smiled, words not finding their way to his lips. He felt cared for and he liked it.

CHAPTER 13

AFTER DINNER the three of them played a game of Monopoly. Reggie and Ana sipped on their wine, while the brilliant teenager whipped both of their asses and laughed as her mother's profits dwindled down to a box of matchsticks.

With the whole weekend to spend together, Ana spent Saturday giving Reggie the tour of all tours. And with Amy-Lynn's high energy level, they opted to spend their Sunday at The Santa Monica Pier. Ana had extended the invitation to Rachel, but she flatly declined. Although Ana was hurt, she didn't hold it against her. She knew Rachel had to work through the situation on her own. In time, she'd be ready to move forward; until then, all Ana could do was love her from afar.

Ana invited Amy-Lynn's friend Jessica along for the day. Amy-Lynn was far more adventurous in her youth than either Reggie or Ana had been. The Ferris wheel was fine, but too many twirling rides and they'd be feeling it come the morning. Instead, the two of them enjoyed the confections and games.

"Why does truck-stop food always taste so damn good?" Reggie asked as he bit into a sloppy chili-cheese dog with more topping than a hotdog.

"Because they're trying to kill us?"

Reggie almost choked on the hotdog. "Maybe, but what a hell of a way to go! This dog is amazing!"

"I'm a sucker for these fish tacos."

"Yeeeeeah..." Reggie scrunched up his nose.

"You like fish, don't you?"

"Tuna, sometimes shrimp, but I'm really a red meat kind of guy."

"Huh. Didn't know that."

"Now if the fish is super deep-fried and smothered in tartar sauce, then bring it on! Otherwise, not so much."

"Well, I will keep that in mind."

Reggie chased his dog down with an extra-large Mountain Dew and wondered if Ruth would kick his ass if she'd seen him. He looked guilty and Ana wondered why.

"What's with the face?" she asked.

"What do you mean?"

"You look guilty."

"I do?"

"Hmm. Now you sound guilty, too."

"Well, if I was honest, I'd be avoiding these dogs a little better than I have this week."

"Oh?"

"Ruth would chew me out for sure."

"Why? You're in good shape."

"I may have kept the weight in check, but that was mostly thanks to Ruth making sure I did. But my cholesterol isn't what it should be."

"I see," said Ana. "Well, the occasional indulgence is fine, just don't make it a regular staple."

"Yeah, I've heard that before."

"What is your cholesterol at, if you don't mind me asking?"

"I got it down to 156."

"From what?"

"174."

"Holy shit!" Ana gasped. "No wonder your wife was so concerned!"

"I know," he said with a downtrodden pout. "But the dogs do taste good."

"The taste of a heart attack won't!" she said.

"Wow," he huffed. "When did you get so preachy?" he mumbled softly, annoyed at her presumptuous statement.

"What?"

"It's lower," he insisted. "Please, let me enjoy my vacation."

"Alright." She felt awkward. "Did I say something wrong?"

He didn't want it to become an argument, so he let it drop. "No, never mind."

"Okay." She got the feeling the topic needed to change. "So, you're here for another week, right?"

"Yes."

"I do have to work it, but you're welcome to dine with us again."

"That would be fine."

He didn't know why he'd gotten so upset with her; he knew she wasn't being preachy. She cared. He knew that. Dismissing his bad attitude on the subject he changed the topic again. They toured the games section, pausing here and there to watch the people pawning for their prizes.

"Oh, geez." Ana paused with a wistful smile.

Reggie found it intriguingly charming and sought an explanation. "What's got your attention?" he asked.

"The frog." She pointed.

"Okay?" Reggie was confused.

"I've got to win that for Rachel," Ana explained. "She loves, loves, loves frogs! I don't know what it is about frogs, but she adores them."

"Go for it!" he told her. He handed her a handful of dollar bills and watched as she tossed the baseballs at the pyramid of ten milk bottles.

Ball number one missed.

Ball number two hit the top two and missed the bottom eight.

Ball number three knocked down five of the bottles.

"Oh, damn it!" she bellowed. "I'll try again." She handed the game's keeper another three dollars and began with three more baseballs.

Ball number one hit all but four of the bottles.

Ball number two took out two more.

Ball number three hit one of the last two, leaving the tenth and final bottle.

"And the lady wins a prize!" announced the gamekeeper.

He handed Ana a string of plastic jewelry and raised a brow. "Are you serious?" she sneered. "I knocked down nine balls and I get this?"

"Dat's right, lady," he replied. "I donnat make dee wules, I only obey dem." His speech was terrible. "Bud, if you like you kin try again."

"Oh, good grief!" She fumbled with her stack of the one-dollar bill and groaned. "How many necklaces do I need to get the frog?"

"You either knock the stack down three times in a row or you play until you have ten of them to get the frog."

"That's highway robbery!" she bitched.

"Here." Reggie said. "Let me."

"Here's the three dollars. Give me the balls," Reggie said stepping in.

The man smiled boastfully. "I love that the men sink dey will do so well. Most make fools of demselves."

"One of them is probably being held on with a magnetized bottom. It's rigged not to fall down unless you hit it just so," he explained to Ana.

"You think you can hit it?"

Reggie winked and said nothing more.

Ball one.

Bam!

He hit the bottom middle bottle and shattered the foundation, knocking all of the bottles to the ground.

The game's keeper's jaw dropped.

Reggie moved to the second stack and pitched again.

Bam!

A second stack tumbled to the ground.

"You must be cheating!" scoffed the man.

"Oh no, sir. I don't cheat." Reggie scoffed. "I'm a lawyer who got himself to Harvard on a baseball scholarship!"

Then he threw the final ball, shattering the bottom bottle and knocking the stack to the ground.

"You cannot cheat!" said the keeper.

"I'd be very careful, sir. You're breaking some laws here and I can prove it. Either hand over the frog or be deported back to your country. I know you're working here illegally."

The man gulped. He sized Reggie up and could see that he was serious. Without any further conflict, he handed them the big frog.

"See now? That's more like it." Reggie took the frog proudly and handed it to Ana, who was somewhat dumbstruck.

"I'm impressed!" she said.

"Me, too," said Reggie. "I haven't thrown a ball like that in years. I think I hurt my shoulder." He winked.

Ana giggled as she accepted the frog and swooned fondly over the man who'd won it so easily.

"By the way...?" she asked.

"Yes?"

"How did you know he was illegally working here?"

"I didn't," Reggie said.

"You bluffed?"

"Uh-huh."

"Damn, you're good!"

Amy-Lynn was impressed when she heard about Reggie's great pitching arm. The frog was huge.

"Rachel's going to love this!" she said.

"I hope so," Ana sighed. "Something's gotta give."

The day ended peacefully and pleasantly. Dinner on the pier as the sunset put the finishing touches on the perfect weekend.

"I wish this didn't have to end," Ana said. "This has been a fabulous weekend!"

"It has, hasn't it?" Reggie agreed. "We can get together again, can't we? I mean before I head back to Pennsylvania?"

"Sure. When do you leave, exactly?"

"Friday at 11 a.m.," he said.

"Wow, that doesn't give us much time. But you are welcome to come to dinner any night this week if you like."

"Yes, I would like that."

Reggie walked the lovely ladies back to their apartment and bid them a good evening. It was late and Ana had an early morning meeting. But she wished she could play hooky again.

Reggie waited outside the building and watched for the apartment light to flick on before leaving. He wanted to go up again, but he was the only one on vacation; for his companions, it was a work and school night. The play would have to be postponed.

CHAPTER 14

IT WAS THURSDAY NIGHT, the night before he would return to Pennsylvania, and he was in agony. Part of him wanted to stay; another part of him was still connected to his love for Ruth. Despite his reservations, he agreed to have dinner one last time with Ana and Amy-Lynn. Rachel reluctantly agreed to meet the man who'd won the fantastic frog, but she was not in the mood to 'give in' easily.

Arriving at the apartment, Reggie waited for the three women to join him in his car. A true gentleman, he opened the door to let Ana and the girls into the car. Rachel tried to be annoyed but was secretly impressed.

"I can do it, sir," she said.

"I'm sure you can," Reggie said. "By all means," he gestured for her to take over, but smiled just enough to let her know he wasn't angry.

"Thanks," Rachel said.

Rachel didn't look like Ana at all. She had long, brownish hair, with multiple streaks of blonde strung through it. She had blaringly bold green eyes and a great figure.

"I'm glad you could join us tonight," Reggie said.

"Thanks," she mumbled.

"Did you thank him for the frog?" Amy-Lynn asked.

"Umm." Rachel felt awkward as she jabbed her elbow into Amy-Lynn's side and gave her 'the death ray look'.

"It's alright, she doesn't have to."

"Yes, Rachel, a thank you would be nice," Ana said.

"I was going to thank him!" she snapped. "I didn't need to be pushed!"

Ana was annoyed that Rachel was being so flippant, but Reggie wasn't offended. "You know what Rachel, I'm happy you like the frog." He smiled into the mirror.

"I do like the frog. It's great. Thank you, Mr. Whitaker."

"My pleasure," he said. Then in an effort to lighten the mood, he blurted out where they were going. "So, have any of you been to One Pico?"

"Wow!" Amy-Lynn gasped. "Jessica's dad took her there once. She said it was very nice!"

"Oh, Reggie," Ana interjected. "It's a bit pricy for four people, don't you think?"

"No worries, already made the reservation," Reggie said.

Rachel was impressed but refrained from saying so.

"Daddy never took us to places like that!"

"Daddy's not rich."

"Girls!" Ana interjected again, knowing a fight would ensue if she didn't.

After being seated, the girls marveled at the elegant decor and lovely ocean view. The sun was setting and the atmosphere was perfect for such a special evening.

"I hate that you're leaving tomorrow, Mr. Whitaker," Amy-Lynn said.

"Me, too. But I do have to get back to my job and I'm certain by now the lawn is in desperate need of cutting."

"Will you be back?" she asked.

Ana looked at Reggie hoping the answer was yes, but she wasn't about to push it.

"I'd like that," he replied.

"When?" Amy-Lynn asked.

"Umm." He didn't know what to say, but he tried to handle it delicately. "I'll have to see what my agenda looks like."

Amy-Lynn accepted the answer, just as his cell phone rang.

Reggie looked at the call display and then said, "I'm sorry ladies, it's my son. I best take this call."

Reggie excused himself and went to a quieter place to answer the phone.

While he was gone, Amy-Lynn asked, "So, how are you going to keep him here, Mom?"

"Amy-Lynn, I can't keep him here."

"You like him, don't you?"

"They're just friends, right mother?" Rachel asked.

"Umm, sure."

"Bull!" Amy-Lynn said. "They are more than friends."

"I don't want to hear it!" Rachel snapped.

"Get over it, Rachel. Mom and dad are done. It's time for Mom to move on!"

"Girls, please!" Ana said firmly. "You're causing a scene and he's coming back. Be civil, ok?"

The girls agreed as Reggie returned to join them.

He looked out the window and marveled for a moment. "I don't know how people get used to those amazing sunsets!" he said. "I've been here two weeks and I'm still amazed."

"It's true, most people take it for granted," Ana said. "Folks just get too busy to take the time."

"I can see that. Life gets hectic."

"So, is everything alright?" Ana asked.

"Oh, the phone call?"

Ana nodded.

"Yes, it's fine. But it appears my son is getting married in three weeks."

"Didn't they just get engaged?" Ana asked.

"Uh-huh."

"Why so quickly?" Rachel asked.

"Well, it appears that Faith is expecting."

"Oh," Ana said.

"Oh, I'm not worried. They've been dating for five years."

"Well, I'm happy for them then," Ana said.

"How many grandkids do you have, Mr. Whitaker?" Rachel asked.

"Three. This will make four."

"How nice!"

CHAPTER 15

DINNER WAS AMAZING – fresh food, great company, a fantastic sunset, it all wrapped up his vacation swimmingly. Driving back to the apartment, the girls in the back didn't say much. The evening was fresh and the beach was quiet.

"Can we take a walk along the beach, Mom?" Amy-Lynn asked.

"Not alone, not at this hour," Ana said.

"We could all go, if you like," Reggie offered.

"That would be nice. It seems so nice out!" Rachel agreed.

"A break from the heat," Ana said. "Let's do it then."

After parking the car near the apartment building, the four of them took a stroll along the beach. Although they couldn't see much, the sounds of singing whales could be heard. The girls were about twenty feet in front of them and burying their toes in the sand as they carried their shoes.

The sound of the whales caught Ana's attention.

"Ah, damn!" groaned Ana. "Every time the whales come near shore, I miss it!"

"They come often?" Reggie asked.

"Well, not super close, but I know my neighbors and many tourists have seen them in the distance," she groaned. "It's one of the reasons I came to the beach apartment."

"I seem to remember you were fond of sea life," Reggie said.

"Yes, I find them amazing!"

"You haven't taken a cruise?"

"No. Carl was scared of boats."

"That's too bad," Reggie said.

"It's on my bucket list," she said.

"Mine, too."

"Really?"

"I didn't think about a bucket list until Ruth died, but when she created hers, I started one, too."

"What's on your list, Reggie?"

"Oh, geez. It's probably silly."

"No, nothing that's important to you can be silly."

"Okay. I'll go first. Then it's your turn, alright?"

"Sure, that's fair."

"I'd like to go on a boat cruise and see the whales, maybe even to Alaska to see a polar bear riding an iceberg, ya know? I'd like to go hiking in the Rockies, take a trip to Africa and go on a safari and I'd like to visit Niagara Falls. Also, take a cross-country trip, Route 66."

"Brilliant!" Ana said.

"Your turn."

"Alright. I'd like to see the girls grow up, find great husbands and give me lots and lots of grandkids. I'd like to go to Europe and just see where my mother and father came from. The whale thing, though, that's right up there on the top!"

"Great dreams!" Reggie said. "Oh, that reminds me! I wanted to ask you something silly."

"What's that?"

"I know this is stupid," he said. "But, well, I want to stay in touch with you better this time."

"Me, too."

"Well, it turns out that my son, the one who's getting married, said I should invite you as my guest."

"Really?"

"That's alright, isn't it? Can you get the time off? I can pay for the flight."

"Oh, it's fine. I am sure I can manage it. I'll have Rachel stay with Amy-Lynn and Chester."

"Great!" He was pleased.

"What's great?" Rachel asked as the girls returned.

"I'm going to Pennsylvania in a few weeks to visit Reggie and to attend his son's wedding."

"Seriously?" Rachel looked unhappy.

"What's wrong with that?" Amy-Lynn asked.

"I thought this was a one-night stand...fling...thing."

"Rachel Marie Johnson!" Ana scolded. "That's rude!"

"I'm sorry, Mom. Mr. Whitaker, I mean you no offense. You're a nice man, but you are not my dad. My dad belongs with my mom. He's just got to get over this mid-life thing, and then he'll be back."

"Rachel, I don't care to discuss this again with you!"

"Well, it's not fair!" Rachel stamped. "I didn't get a say in this!"

"Rachel, I need you to understand."

"I don't want to understand! Daddy made a mistake and you won't forgive him!" she shouted. "You told us we needed to be forgiving. Why can't you forgive him?"

"Rachel, I don't wish to discuss this now."

"Then don't!" she shouted. "I'm going to Daddy's!"

"You can't go running to Daddy every time you don't get your way, Rachel," Amy-Lynn said.

"Butt out, Amy!"

"Girls! That's enough!" Ana shouted.

"I'm out of here!"

Rachel stormed back to the apartment and left the three of them on the beach.

"Reggie, I'm sorry."

"It's alright."

"I..."

"I'll call you when I get home, alright?"

"Alright." Ana was angry with Rachel, sad that Reggie was gone and embarrassed by the display of craziness he'd witnessed his last night in Santa Monica.

CHAPTER 16

REGGIE COULD NOT SLEEP. He paced the floor restlessly and then tried relaxing on the balcony with a tea, but nothing was working. A sleeping pill wasn't a good idea; he had to be out of the room early and didn't want to risk oversleeping.

His mind was obsessed. Obsessed with Ana. Obsessed with Ruth. Obsessed with life. He knew he cared about Ana still. He'd always cared about her. But he also loved Ruth and he'd had a great life with her. Why did he feel so guilty? He had no idea. Nobody would judge him for moving on; it'd been a few months since Ruth passed away and he was an attractive and eligible man.

In talking with William about Ana, he'd had a lot of support. Reggie's kids knew he wouldn't cheat on their mother and they didn't feel that he was betraying her memory. They knew how much he'd loved her; they never had reason to question it. Seeing him move on would make them all happy.

Then as the night gave way to morning, there was a knock at his hotel door.

"Five a.m.?" he groaned. "My wake-up call was for seven," he mumbled to himself. "I'm up already," he shouted.

"Reggie?"

He knew the voice and immediately opened the door.

"Ana? What are you doing here?"

"I'm sorry. I probably woke you," she said. "I just didn't want you to go before I could say goodbye one last time."

"Oh, thanks. I'm glad you came by."

"I know it's stupid. I'm an old woman who's acting like a fifteen-year-old girl."

"It's not stupid at all Ana. I'm glad you came by."

"Not just saying that, are you?"

"Not at all," he said. "Breakfast?"

"Sure."

"I'm going to freshen up first," he said, grabbing his toiletries. "That alright?"

"Of course," she said. "Shall I order breakfast?"

"That would be great!" he said. Then he walked into the washroom and proceeded with his morning routine.

Ana was already dressed for work, but she wanted desperately to play hooky. At least until Reggie left for the airport.

'No Ana, he's got to go to Pennsylvania. You might as well just face it – the rendezvous will have to wait, yet again.' She sighed. 'Even with the wedding next month, this long-distance thing is going to get tricky.'

She ordered eggs Benedict, home fries, toast, coffee, and orange juice, and sat on the balcony watching the city come to life while she waited for the food. From the balcony, she could hear the bellowing sounds of whales in the distance. The sun illuminated the surface of the water just enough for her to see a few spouts of spray as it burst from the blowhole.

"Oh my God!" she gasped with her eyes full of wonder.

Reggie, who'd exited the washroom undetected, heard her exclamation and approached curiously. "What is it?" he asked, startling her.

"Oh gracious, you scared the crap out of me."

"Sorry."

"It's fine. But Reggie, look!" She pointed eagerly at the patch of spraying mammals in the distance.

"Is that...?"

"Whales!" She was like a 5-year-old in a pet store. "Oh God, they're beautiful!"

Reggie was equally impressed. He stood behind her, smelling of Old Spice body wash. She didn't dare take her attention off the whales; his presence was making her horny and she wasn't about to let him know that.

"They sure are impressive," he said.

Then suddenly, from the deep blue the large creature leaped from the ocean and flopped its body down upon the surface with a humongous splash.

"Oh my God!" they exclaimed in unison.

"That was freaking amazing!" Reggie said.

"This is unbelievable!" Ana added. "You must be good luck or something. I've been living by the ocean for months, been near the ocean most of my life, and I've never seen a whale like this."

"Do you know what kind it was?"

"Humpback, I think." she smiled. "They don't often come so close to shore here. This is truly an exquisite moment."

"Makes for a fantastic send-off!" he said. "If only I'd had my camera handy."

"Moments like that are hard to capture. My mind will have to hold on to this image for me," Ana said.

The morning glow highlighted Ana's beauty and Reggie felt compelled to kiss her. But it was too painful. He couldn't get past his devotion to Ruth. And knowing that the distance thing hadn't worked in the past ate at him.

But, maybe, for the moment he could just hold her.

He wrapped his arms around her shoulders and held her gently while they continued to marvel at the display of the big blue creatures. Ana didn't say anything, but accepted his embrace willingly, wishing it would last forever.

CHAPTER 17

REGGIE BOARDED the plane and took the long flight home, feeling irked that he'd had to leave the woman he'd cared about so long ago. But he knew life in Pennsylvania was waiting for him and he had clients who needed his expertise. His business savvy and skill had been honed to an art. Companies big and small called on him whenever their businesses needed a boost or legal nurturing. Word on the street was that Reginald Whitaker was a force to be reckoned with.

Pulling into his driveway, Reggie was happy to see that someone had been around to care for his property. His yard was green, cut, and the flower garden Ruth spent so much time on had been taken care of as well. He felt loved.

Then he went to the front door and noted that the newspapers and mail had been collected for him; another sign that he was loved. It felt good.

As he turned the key to the front door and entered the abandoned house, he smiled. Everything was in order. No dust, it smelled clean, and the mail was stacked neatly on the small table. He was greeted by a familiar voice.

"Hi, dad!" shouted Amber as she came around the corner.

"Hi, sweetheart," he said, giving his daughter a hug. "Did you do all this, Amber?"

"Yep," she said. "I figured you needed the boost to keep going."

"You are so much like your mother," he said.

"I take that as a compliment," she replied.

"It's true."

"So, tell me about your trip," she said. "I've made tea."

"Tea sounds great."

Reggie removed his shoes and carried his baggage to the laundry room. Some serious catching up was in order. The crisp new suit caught Amber's eye.

"Nice suit, dad," she said. "I didn't think you were taking a suit though."

"I bought it while I was there."

"Really nice. Bet you looked sharp in it."

Amber poured them both a cup of tea, added milk and one sugar, and handed one to her father. She could see that he was happier than he was when he left.

"You look refreshed," she said.

"I am," he replied. Looking around the kitchen, he could see the many reflections of Ruth's time in the home. She'd been infatuated with gingerbread men and they were everywhere. The cookie jar, the utensil container, the oven mitts, the table cloth, and even the salt and pepper shakers were gingerbread men. If he thought about it hard enough he could smell the fresh batch of cookies coming out of the oven while she happily decorated the cool batch. He sighed.

"I miss her, too, dad," Amber said.

"I know you do, dear."

"But she wouldn't want us to sit here and mope. She loved life too much for that."

"I know it. She lived every moment for joy. Every moment for you kids, for me, even the neighbors knew she could be counted on."

Amber smiled warmly as she sipped her tea and said, "So, tell me...who's Ana?"

"I see you've been talking to William."

"Yes. He said she's coming to the wedding."

"She is."

"How did you meet?"

"We were in high school together," he told her.

"Your prom date?"

"Yeah, how'd you know?"

"I've seen your pictures."

"We're just good friends," he said.

"Who are you telling? Me or yourself?"

"What do you mean?"

"Do you care for her?"

"I don't want to push things."

"Does she like you?"

"I expect she does, but I don't know how much."

"You were deeply in love once, I heard that."

"From who?"

"Aunt Shirley told me about Ana years ago. When I stumbled on the prom picture at Nana's house I asked."

"I hadn't seen her in over thirty years. We hadn't talked since my second year at Harvard. So many years have gone by."

"But it's your first love, right dad?"

"Yes, but..."

"But nothing, Dad. I know you loved Mom. Nobody

would dispute that. She's been dead for a few months now and you have the chance to love again. I say go for it!"

Reggie almost choked on his tea. "Amber, I'm surprised to hear you say that!"

"Why? Robert, William, and I want you to be happy. We know Mom will be a part of your life forever, but if Ana, or anyone for that matter, can make you as happy as Mom did again, then we want that for you."

"I can't believe how grown-up you're being about this."

"Daddy, I am grown-up. I am married and have two daughters, a mortgage, and a career in the works."

"I know, but I can't help but see you as my little pig-tailed girl still." He looked into the backyard at the tree-house he'd built many years ago and pictured his kids climbing around inside. "I can still see you climbing that ladder. William was practically half-monkey, but it took you a little longer."

"I know," she said. "I was awkward."

"No, not awkward," Reggie said. "Methodical. You didn't do anything without thinking things through first. You're still like that."

"I guess I get that from you," she said. "Mom was a little more spontaneous."

"You can say that again!" he snickered. "I remember when she brought home that silly ceramic horse from the garage sale. That thing is still a big focal point in the yard."

Amber giggled. "She was always shopping for something."

"The more unique the better."

"But she was frugal!"

"Except for gingerbread ornaments," he said as he picked up the salt shaker.

"Well, when it came to gingerbread and Christmas, she was more like one of my girls than she was a mom."

"One of the many things I cherished about her. She was passionate, through and through."

CHAPTER 18

BACK IN HER APARTMENT, Ana had been dealing with Rachel's attitude. She'd come and go, spending many nights with her father, who repeatedly ignored his daughter in favor of his girlfriend of the night. But Rachel was adamant that her father would come around and that things would be the way they'd been before. In the meantime, Amy-Lynn showed eager enthusiasm. She liked Reggie. He was good to her mother and she really liked how happy he made Ana. She'd always seek information on the daily messages Reggie sent her mother.

"What'd he say today, Mom?" she asked.

"Just business."

"And the wedding plans, how are they going?"

"Okay, I guess." Ana liked that Amy-Lynn was so receptive, but didn't want her to end up being bitter at her own father.

While Amy-Lynn did agree to make amends with Carl, she was not about to let him hurt her mother again. Reggie seemed great and she said so. Carl showed a modicum amount of interest in the girls, but his mid-life crisis was getting to be more than Amy-Lynn could tolerate.

Ana did not permit Amy-Lynn to speak poorly of her father, despite her own ill feelings. She did, however, allow her to vent when she needed to. She understood that Carl's behavior was less than appropriate, but she knew better than to put him down in front of them.

As Ana and Amy-Lynn were enjoying their Saturday brunch, they were interrupted by a buzz at the door.

"Hello?" Amy-Lynn replied.

"Hey Aims, it's me, Em."

"Hurray!" she shouted happily. "Mom. It's Emily. I hope she's got the baby!"

A few seconds later Emily stepped off the elevator with the spy Amy-Lynn watching carefully through the peephole. "Hurray!" she cheered. "She brought Cayson!"

"Oh, good," Ana said.

From the moment Cayson was born, Ana had adapted a new passion: grandchildren. She loved being a grandmother and told everyone she knew that it was the best experience of her life. Cayson was nearly 15 months old, but they hadn't seen him in about three months.

"Oh, he's walking!" Amy-Lynn applauded.

Emily lived in Thousand Oaks, which was just under an hour away, with her husband and son.

Amy-Lynn eagerly opened the door. "Hi, sis!" she shouted.

Her big burst of energy surprised Cayson and he fell down on his diapered bottom.

"Oh!" Amy-Lynn gasped. "I'm sorry. I didn't mean to scare him!"

"It's fine, Aims. He's still a little tipsy at times," Emily explained. "Good to see you!" The girls gave one another a hug and then entered the apartment.

Ana was all smiles when Cayson walked into the room. "Oh my, he's getting so big!" Ana scooped him up and gave him a great big hug. "It's great to see you, Emily! I didn't know you two were coming. Can you stay for dinner?"

"Yes, we can stay," she said.

"Everything alright?" Ana asked.

Suddenly the look on Emily's face changed. The look of deep sorrow and fear ran across her face as the tears began to well up.

"Oh, Mommy." Then like a bursting dam, the flood of tears began to rush forward. Ana and Amy-Lynn were dumbfounded.

"Oh my God, Emily!" Amy-Lynn gasped.

"Emily, what's happened?" Ana asked.

Cayson, who'd been sitting on Ana's lap, was getting restless.

"Sit still Cayson," Emily said impatiently.

"Here, let me take him to my room. We'll watch Blue's Clues or something. You two talk," Amy-Lynn took the baby from Ana's arms and carried him to her room. She looked back briefly with concern for her big sister.

"Thanks, Aims." Emily forced a smile at her son and

sister. Then she looked back at her mother, whose face cried for an explanation.

"What's happened, Emily?" Ana asked again.

"It's Jack."

Ana's "mama bear" began to emerge as she prepared to listen to how he'd hurt her daughter.

"What happened?"

Emily proceeded to roll up her sleeves and showed her two large bruises.

"Oh my God!" Ana was horrified. "Did he do this?"

Emily nodded.

"Please tell me this is the first time?"

Emily shook her head, shamefully.

"How long has this been going on?"

"Since I became pregnant with Cayson," she said.

"Dear God, Emily! Why didn't you say something? Your father and I would have ripped his head off!"

"I know you would have. I just hoped it would stop. Stupid, I guess." Emily's lip began to quiver again. "I was hoping I could stay here for a few days while I..."

"You can stay as long as you need."

Then Emily started to cry again.

"Is there more?"

"I'm not even going to be able to help with the finances. I lost my job when Jack made me take two weeks off. And now..." She began to rub her tummy gently.

"Are you expecting again?"

"Yes. Twelve weeks."

Ana smiled. "Well, I am sorry you have had to go through this, but I am glad to have another grandchild."

"I can't support us!"

"Don't you worry about that right now? You let me worry about that. When you're back on your feet, then we'll talk. For now, let's get you and that dear boy settled in, okay?"

"Thanks, Mom."

Ana embraced her daughter and held her with compassion and love.

CHAPTER 19

IT WAS EASIER this time for them to keep in touch. Between Facebook, email, and texting, it had become much easier and more efficient to communicate long-distance.

With his kids' encouragement, Reggie began to open the door a little and began letting Ana re-enter his heart. While they kept the communication simple and unassuming, there were little flirtations passed back and forth.

Although Reggie hadn't been accustomed to text messaging or chatting too much – most of his communication had been on the professional level – he soon caught on to the Internet jargon and became a master of ttyl, bbfn, and, of course, the winky face. Still, it was simple flirtations they shared.

He often thought of their last breakfast with the whales leaping in the morning's light. He remembered their walk along the beach and the pleasure he had in winning the frog for Rachel.

The time went quickly and both of them were glad. They'd shared their tales back and forth over the various lines of communication and counted the days to their reunion. Now, Ana got on a plane and flew to see Reggie once again.

Emily had stayed with Amy-Lynn and her son at the apartment, but Rachel was still off and on about her feelings. Ana didn't press the issue with her anymore, but through the advice of a great confidant, she decided to let Rachel sort things out for herself.

Reggie waited for Ana at the airport, his heart fluttering when they announced the arrival of her flight. He waited eagerly as he watched the passengers de-board. Each time a woman with shoulder-length blonde hair came into view, he felt a rush and surge of joy, but then it wasn't her.

"Damn," he cussed. "Where is she?"

"I'm behind you, silly!" Her voice surprised him and he whirled around suddenly.

"How'd you get behind me?"

"I came in that door," she giggled.

He looked back and forth a few times at the two doors. "Oh." He felt silly. He'd been staring at the wrong door the whole time. Then, he took a good look at her and smiled. She was wearing a red, long-sleeved blouse and a white sweater, blue jeans; her hair was held back by a pair of sunglasses. He was smitten.

"You look amazing!" he told her.

"Thank you. So do you," she said.

The two of them smiled and then greeted with a hug.

"How was your flight?" he asked.

"The flight was easy enough, but I got stuck beside a chainsaw!"

"Chainsaw?"

"He snored so loud the other passengers were giving me looks of concern. I finally stuck my daughter's iPod thingy into my ears and drowned out the snoring with Charlotte Church. I'd never used an iPod thingy before, but I'm glad she lent it to me."

"Well, sounds to me like you're in need of a good dinner out then, right?"

It was only one in the afternoon, but she agreed. A nice dinner out would be just right. They made their way to his car and proceeded to his house. She marveled at the city sights and wondered if she'd get a ten-cent tour as well.

Trying to hint that she'd like a tour, she asked, "So that's City Hall, is it?"

"Yes," he replied. "You've never had a tour of Philly?"

"Never been, Reg."

"Well, well, well... Then I guess we better take care of that now, huh?"

"I'd love it!"

Reggie stopped at a Speedway, filled the tank with gas and then gave Ana the tour she'd been looking for. They stopped at the Declaration House, the National Constitution Centre, Independence Hall, and, of course, the Liberty Bell.

"This is amazing!" she said as she snapped a dozen pictures of the bell. "So much history here!"

"I know, each building has a story to tell it seems," he replied.

"I'd almost forgotten what it was like in this climate. So refreshing!"

"We have smog."

"Yeah, but you can't actually see it!" she said. "There are days when it's so thick in L.A. that you can't see the beach from my balcony."

"That is pretty bad, isn't it?"

She nodded.

"I got to make one quick stop if you don't mind."

"Of course not, it's fine."

Reggie pulled into the parking lot of his building. "Would you like to see where I work?"

"Sure," she replied.

They made their way to his office and she marveled at the antique artifacts and architecture that surrounded her every step of the way. As a marketing designer, the beauty of these pieces really intrigued her.

Then, as they went into his office he said, "Have a seat. I've just got to check something in my inbox. I was expecting a package. My assistant is on vacation and the temp isn't as familiar with the routine as I'd hoped she'd be."

"I'm familiar with that dilemma," Ana said. "Kat was on maternity leave last year and I was lost! I didn't realize how amazing she was at her job until I had to bring on a replacement. I told her if she had any more kids, I would hire a nanny to sit with her at the desk."

He chuckled as he acknowledged and then returned to the stack of papers. Finally, he picked up a manila envelope and smiled. "I think this is it." He grabbed his letter opener and cut it open.

Then, he carefully slipped his hand inside and pulled out the spiral-bound package. "Ah," he said. "This is it!"

"Good news?"

"I hope so." Reggie began to read it and suddenly cheered, "Yes!"

"Wow, it must be good news."

"Got a huge client! Huge, huge, huge. I was waiting all month for confirmation. This client will keep Randy and I very comfortable!"

"I got ya," she said. "I always get excited when I get a big client. It's like being a child all over again. Hell, I've been doing this job for twenty years and I still get star-struck when a celeb contacts me."

"Oh shit, that's right," he said. "You work with the stars sometimes, don't you?"

"Sometimes, yes."

"Amazing."

"No, not always. Some of them can be pretty demanding," she said.

"That ruins the buzz then, doesn't it?"

"Sometimes," she agreed. "Some are amazing though."

Reggie took Ana to the house to freshen up, and she was immediately in love with his former wife. Her ability to create mood with artifacts and collectibles impressed her. Ana secretly snooped a bit, like any woman would, and marveled at the history and story the house told.

Reggie showed her to her room and then left her to

freshen up while he worked on his new contract for an hour before dinner. As she unpacked her things, she looked at the photos on the dressers and wall. Reggie and Ruth loved their family; it was obvious.

After exchanging her red sweater for her red dress, she returned to the main level of the house and sought out her host.

Reggie was deep in thought as she entered his office space. "Hi," she said softly.

"Oh, damn!" he scoffed. "I didn't realize it had gotten so late!"

"Happens to me all the time," she confessed.

"Bet you're hungry, huh?"

"I am."

"Now that I think about it, I am, too."

"Do you know what you want?"

"Well, I am in Philly…"

"Oh, please say Philly cheesesteak, please say Philly cheesesteak." He looked like a five-year-old looking for his Happy Meal.

"Actually, that is what I had in mind."

"Hurray!" he cheered.

"But wait. What about your cholesterol?"

"I'll have a double batch of oats for breakfast tomorrow, okay?"

She smiled. "Okay." She grabbed her purse and followed Reggie back to his car.

CHAPTER 20

REGGIE AND ANA drove to University City where they selected their dinner destination. They chose to dine at a popular truck stop that delivered the tastiest, messiest food possible.

"Fancy, huh?" asked Reggie.

"Five star all the way!" she said. "Just to my liking."

"Mine, too."

"With all the celebs and first-class people I meet, I am always drawn back to the paper-napkin, messy-faced diners."

"There is something soothing about it, isn't there?"

"Sure is," she agreed.

The two of them walked for a while down the street, quietly enjoying each other's company; neither spoke much at all. Reggie, however, could tell that Ana had something on her mind. He sought to discover the nature of her consumed thoughts.

"What's on your mind?" he asked.

"What do you mean?" She had hoped he hadn't noticed.

"Something's been on your mind all evening, hasn't it?" he asked.

"That obvious?"

He nodded gently.

"It's Em, my eldest."

"Oh?"

"She's going through a hard time," she explained. Reggie nodded understandingly and she continued to tell him about the abuse, the pregnancy, and their living situation. The apartment would not house that many people, so moving was imminent.

"I hate bastards who hurt women!" he groaned. "Although I'm not a family lawyer, many of my Barr colleagues have seen some incredible situations!"

"I bet. I just don't like to see her in pain."

"No parent likes to see their child hurting. It's terrible, but you are doing the right thing."

"I hope so. I know she loved her independence. She's a strong person."

"She can still be strong, but right now she must concentrate on her health and her children. Jack is not good for her health and certainly not for the kids."

"Well, she said he hadn't touched Cayson."

"He doesn't have to. Cayson sees it and hears it. It hurts him in a different way. Besides, Ana, if I know you if that man had laid one finger on the baby...'

"You'd be bailing me out of jail."

"Precisely!"

"Thanks for understanding. I worry about her. I worry about David over in Afghanistan. I worry about Rachel and how she's handling the divorce. And Amy-Lynn."

"Ha! That girl's not afraid of anything or anyone!"

Ana snickered. "You noticed, huh?"

"Couldn't miss that!"

"She's tough, but she's still frustrated with her father. He's simply become obtuse about their relationship. Like it doesn't matter."

"That's got to be hard on her."

"It is."

Reggie put his arm around her shoulder and pulled her closer. They walked side-by-side, feeling the passion of each person's woes and joys.

"Reggie, there was something else I had on my mind. But I don't know how to bring it up," she said.

"What is it?"

"It's about Ruth."

"What about her?"

"I can tell by the way the house looks, and the garden, that she was a very doting wife. She took care of things and I can tell she did a great job taking care of you."

"She did. She was an amazing woman."

"I can tell."

"What's the problem?"

"Well, we have a rather quirky history — you and I — but you've had such a wonderful history with Ruth. I just don't know if..."

"What are you getting at Ana?"

At this point, she wished she hadn't opened this can of worms. What had she said anything at all? "I feel silly."

Reggie stopped walking and turned to face Ana, grabbing her shoulders to create an eye-to-eye stand. "Ana, what's bothering you?"

"I wonder if you're even ready to... I mean... Am I a substitute now? Oh, shit. I'm stupid!" She was annoyed with herself. She'd been second-guessing the connection they had and hoped she wasn't deceiving herself or forcing

Reggie to move on. He'd loved Ruth so much and so deeply; while their childhood love was real, it had been a long time ago. Maybe she was seeing something that wasn't there.

"Ana, are you having second thoughts?" he asked.

"No. I'm not. But I can't even come close to being your Ruth. She was a lovely lady, but I am not crafty at all. I kill plants. I'm not a great cook and I don't like gingerbread."

"Are you afraid that my feelings for Ruth have shaded my feelings for you?"

She shrugged.

"Ana, we have a history — you and I — and I know that my love for Ruth was real. It still is. That will never change. But I am capable of loving again. I loved you before, but things weren't meant to be back then. Now..."

"Now, what?"

"Ana, I admit, I, too, have had some concerns and questions about this 'thing' we've got going on here."

"You have?"

"Silly, I guess. I felt, and sometimes kick myself for feeling it still, that I am betraying Ruth's memory by moving on."

"Do you feel that way?"

"Only sometimes. But it's just a question of my insecurities. Not a question of my feelings for you."

"I don't want to be a substitute, Reg."

"You're not. You're someone I loved once and never really stopped loving. Where ever this goes, I'm ready to follow it. Aren't you?"

"Yes, I'm ready. And scared."

"As am I Ana. As am I."

"Silly, isn't it?"

"Maybe, but I decided that regardless of where this

'thing' goes, I'm ready for the ride and the commitment it takes to give it a good run."

"I'm glad, Reggie."

"You're as beautiful to me now as you were three decades ago. You've become an incredible woman and I'm star-struck that you and I got this second chance."

"Me, too."

"No matter what Ana, I'm ready to see what happens next."

"Can I ask you something personal?"

"Sure?"

"Can I know Ruth, too?"

"What?"

"I'm wondering if you'd let me know more about her."

Reggie looked confused.

"Not to bring up the pain, but I'd love to know more about the woman who kept you happy all these years."

Reggie smiled; he understood her sincerity. "Sure," he said. "What do you want to know?"

The two of them spent the last hour talking about the 30-year history of Reggie and Ruth. Their memories were full of joy, blessing, and even some sorrow. But Ana encouraged the conversation, intrigued to know more about Reggie and his life with Ruth.

Ana smiled and embraced the tales as she determined that in another life and time she and Ruth might have been friends. It equally fascinated her that they were quite different in some ways, but the things that Reggie loved about Ruth were also true of Ana's personality and character. Love was beginning to grow more between the two and Ana welcomed it.

CHAPTER 21

IT WAS the wedding rehearsal for William and Faith's wedding and Ana had not yet met his family. Gathered in the sanctuary, Reggie's children stared curiously as he walked in with Ana by his side. Amber's girls were playing around with their baskets and bouquets, while the adults were discussing the ceremonial order.

As she and Reggie entered, the room got quiet and Ana began to feel awkward. However, she gracefully accepted the transition and moved forward with as much confidence as she could muster. *'If I can speak to a room full of prospective investors, I can certainly enter a room full of Reggie's loved ones,'* she thought to herself.

Amber was the first to approach. "Hello," she said. "You must be Ana."

"I am," Ana replied. "I know you're Amber. I recognize you from the photos in your father's house."

"Yeah, Mom was a big picture junky," Amber giggled.

"I am sorry for your loss, dear," Ana said. While she was interested in Reggie, she wouldn't demean the memory of

Ruth. Ruth had been a great person and she recognized that.

"Thank you," replied Amber. Then, she gently patted Ana's arm as she led her to the midst of the strangers. "Come."

Ana walked nervously, feeling the questions that surrounded her imposition.

Faith, the young bride and mother-to-be, looked radiant. Her youthful zest was apparent and her love for William showed in her smile. Robert's wife, Nora, sat in a pew carefully nursing the infant beneath a draped blanket, while Robert prepared to take his place beside his brother.

"Hey everyone," Amber burbled, "This is Ana. Ana, this is everyone. This is Kailey and Kelsey, the prettiest girls in town," Amber said, introducing her daughters. "Nora's there with the baby. This is William and his bride, Faith. And this is Robert. Also, this is Faith's family, Betty and John Dawson, the maid of honor Laurie, bridesmaids Jessie and Elle, and Phillip. Faith's brother."

As Amber concluded the introductions, the smiles and welcomes followed. Ana wasn't discarded as intrusive but received warmly. It made her feel good. She took a seat beside Nora and the baby and watched quietly as the bridal party rehearsed the wedding.

Nora immediately took to Ana, and once the baby was fed Ana was granted a moment of cuddling with the infant. The baby's soft, warm head nuzzled cozily beneath her neck; the sweet baby smell wafted up to her nose. Her heart pitter-pattered fondly as she patted his little bottom and rocked him gently.

"You're good with kids," Nora said. "I can tell."

"Thanks. I have a few."

"Four, right?"

"Yes, that's right."

"Reggie's talked a bit about you. He really seemed to adore, uh, what's the name? Oh, yes. Amy-Lou?"

"Amy-Lynn."

"Right."

"Yes, they hit it off swimmingly!"

"Well, I know it must be hard to move back into Reggie's life with everything that's happened, but if I know Reggie, he wouldn't have brought you around if there'd been anything 'off' about you."

"Thanks. I think?"

"Honestly, knowing him the few years I have, if he loves you, he loves you all the way. Ruth was his world and I didn't know if we'd ever see him smile again. You've brought that back. We are thrilled."

Ana was thrilled, too. She hadn't 'moved in' to gain their approval; she loved him and she knew it. Somewhere down deep, he loved her, too, and she was patient enough to let what was going to blossom with time.

As she and Nora spoke quietly amongst themselves, she caught a glimpse of Reggie's face as he looked over to give her a warm smile. It felt good and she wanted it to last.

William stood proudly as the sound of the violins began to announce the entrance of his bride. She walked gracefully and radiated an aura of beauty. And although the tiny rounded belly was beginning to appear, it was elegantly masked by the beautiful bouquet of flowers.

Ana enjoyed the ceremony but loved it even more when Reggie's son spoke his personally written vows.

"With Mom's passing, I remember watching my father and knowing the pain he felt. But even with that pain, I wanted what he had with Mom. Their love was true and pure, unwavering, and it's with this in mind that I wrote my vows," William said. "I, William, promise to cherish you, love you, and be your confidant through every step of our lives together. I promise to be the man you deserve and the father our kids will need. I promise to do my best to put the seat down-" the crowd chuckled, "-and above all, I promise to love you until the day we die."

Reggie wiped a tear from his eye, along with many others in the room. William and Faith were starting a family in a rather non-traditional way, but there was no question that their love was real. Ana wished them all the best and couldn't help but recall the 'better days' she had with Carl. Still, wiping her own pettiness aside, she chose to focus on Reggie's family for the day and determined to allow things to be as they would.

With the reverend's conclusion, William and Faith were pronounced: "husband and wife" and the crowd applauded appropriately.

"Do you remember being in love like that?" one woman asked another in the row behind Reggie and Ana.

"No," scoffed one. "But if I had, I'd never let it go. Never!"

Ana agreed; real love, true love, is precious and should never be taken for granted. Although Reggie's love had died and Ana's love had perished at the hands of a young jezebel harlot, she agreed that love was precious and she hoped Faith and William would have a wonderful life together.

Secretly, and selfishly, she wished the same for herself, too.

At the reception, Robert proposed a toast that suited the couple, as did a number of other adoring souls.

Dinner had been sensational and, without a doubt, expensive. Yet, as five-star as the wedding might have been, they kept it relatively simple and intimate.

Then, with the music beginning, the first dance of the night began and romance was in the air. William moved his pregnant bride gracefully around the floor and looked endlessly into her eyes. Locked in one another's embrace, the happy couple appeared to be lost in their world.

"They look wonderful together!" Ana said.

"William has a lovely bride, doesn't he?"

"Indeed. Not to mention your next grandchild!"

"Yes, I do love being a grandpa!"

No sooner had he said it that tiny Kelsey tugged on his arm. "Grandpa," she said.

"Yes, Kelsey?"

"Can you pour me some punch?"

"Sure, I'll get you some punch." He began to lead the child to the red punch, but the child stopped.

"No, Papa," she insisted. "I want that one!"

The bowl of purple punch was pretty. It flowed elegantly through a series of cherubs and did appear tempting, but it was not for children.

"I'm sorry, Kelsey," he said. "That punch is for adults."

"But I want the purple punch!" she squawked.

Reggie knew how to fix the problem. "Tell you what," he said. "I have an idea." Then, Reggie went to the liquor bar and spoke for a moment with the bartender. With a wink and smile, he took a small bottle of blue food coloring and began to dribble drops of it into the red punch. Then, with a few stirs, the whole thing was purple.

"Grandpa! You made it purple!" she cheered.

Ana smiled. Reggie had become a hero to his granddaughter; his joy was in knowing he'd made his precious granddaughter smile. Ana's heart fluttered with sensual fascination.

As Kelsey sat down with her purple juice, the D.J. changed the music once again. "I Only Have Eyes for You" by the Flamingos began to play and suddenly Ana shuttered.

"Oh my God!" she gasped silently.

She whirled around quickly and looked at the D.J., then suddenly felt a warm hand set upon her shoulder. Then she turned back around and looked deeply into the bright blue eyes of Reggie and felt virtually paralyzed. *'Does he remember?'* she wondered.

"This was our song, wasn't it?" he asked.

Ana's eyes began to tear up slightly as she nodded, not finding the words to reply.

"The last dance of our prom." He looked intently into her eyes and smiled. "You do remember, right?"

She nodded as she swallowed a persistent lump. "I do remember, Reggie."

"Shall we?" he asked as he held out his hand in gesture, inviting hers to join his.

Like a child lost in a Cinderella story, Ana placed her hand into Reggie's and willingly and timidly allowed him to lead her to the dance floor.

Reggie walked her to the center of the floor and for the moment, their own serenity began to unfold. Reggie's kids watched painfully, but approvingly. They were happy to see their dad happy again, but they could not forget their mother. It was bittersweet, the erotic moment unfolding as the music played on and on.

The lights danced in a brilliant display upon the floor as Ana rested her head against Reggie's chest and he rested his chin upon her hair. Her hair smelled good; her skin was soft and warm. His heartbeat steadily as they moved gracefully around and round.

As the song continued, he gazed into her eyes and she found herself reliving their prom and wishing somehow that the night would last forever.

Ana felt her heart skipping as her feet began to dance upon the clouds of heaven. Reggie's strong and loving arms held her with pure masculinity and the salt-and-pepper flecks in his hair seemed to blink with approval.

Gently, as they turned, Reggie placed his hand upon her cheek and caressed it softly. His own heart was melting like candle wax. The passion of the moment overwhelmed them; the crowd found joy in seeing Reggie's newfound life.

The man had only months earlier all but given up on life, but with the love of a very special lady the life he'd lost when Ruth died had been restored; the joy was shared by all who admired their hearts of silver.

CHAPTER 22

THE WEDDING CONCLUDED and the crowd slowly dwindled down, leaving just a few behind. Gary had taken the girls home while Amber helped collect the rental tuxes to be returned. Reggie and Ana sat quietly together, enjoying one another over some bubbly and nearly forgetting the world around them.

"You two looked amazing out there!" Robert said.

"Thanks, son," Reggie said. "I hope it didn't bother you."

"It did and didn't," he confessed. "I'm glad you found love again. You deserve it. And Ana, you're a great person, I can tell. But I still..." Robert choked a bit on his words.

"You miss your mother," Ana said. "I expected that. Know this, Robert: at no time do I ever intend to take her place. I honor her life because I can tell she was a great person by the people you turned out to be. She'd be proud, I am confident of that."

"Thanks, Ana." Robert's eyes were misty, but he proudly contained his emotions.

Being a gracious woman, Ana stood and looked Robert

in the eye with sincerity and compassion. Without a word she simply offered a hug to the young man. Although Robert had always been a hard-ass and was determined to always be the strong one, something in him still ached deeply. He missed his mother and Ana could see that in his eyes.

Robert accepted the hug; at first, it was simply to be polite, but something in her embrace broke the dam and suddenly his heart burst wide open and he began to sob like a child. Reggie's heart broke, but Ana didn't let the moment pass without allowing the bottled-up Robert to release his pain on her shoulder.

The beautiful embrace of two soon became three as Reggie joined Ana and his eldest son. Amber, who'd caught the show, couldn't restrain herself and suddenly she was making the huddle number four. One by one, those who remained felt the desperation and healing of the family. There wasn't a dry eye among them.

Although Faith's family might have reacted oddly to so many tears at their daughter's wedding, they understood their pain. It was still fresh, and all they could do was melt into one another with tears. Ana stood at the center of the huddle, strong as she could be for the family she'd been learning to love.

As the tears began to finally dry up, they pulled back one-by-one and looked at Ana with amazement.

"How'd you know?" Robert asked.

"I sensed it, I guess."

"You're amazing," Amber said. "You must have felt awkward. I'm sorry if you did. We didn't mean to make you feel bad."

"You didn't. Not at all. I'm happy to be here for you, in the huge shadow of a wonderful woman!"

"Oh, God! You're gonna make me cry again!" Robert said.

"I am simply honored." Ana's tender smile and warmth melted the family through and through, and although William was away with his new bride, Robert and Amber knew he'd agree. Although Ana would not replace their mother, she had undoubtedly become a wonderful icon in their lives.

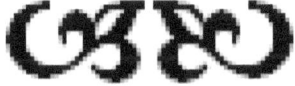

Riding in the back of the limo back to his home, Reggie and Ana sat quietly holding hands. Ana was tired but exhilarated, and Reggie was increasingly amazed by this woman. She was so strong and beautiful. He'd done something right, he figured. How else could he have been loved by two women as amazing as Ruth and Ana? Blessed not once, but twice. No man should be so lucky, but he was glad he'd been chosen to receive this joy he'd found.

"You were amazing tonight, Ana," he said softly.

"You were amazing. You're a great dancer."

"I'm not talking about the dancing, although that was electrifying. The way you cared for my family." His eyes filled with tears once again. "You took care of them...and me."

"Glad I could."

"Do you know how amazing you are?"

Ana looked at Reggie with girlish wonder and humbly shrugged it off.

"Ana..." Reggie's heart began to beat faster as the flood of feelings began to overshadow all sorrows. "I..." He couldn't speak but looked at her with bewilderment. The lights of the street danced upon her face and twinkled in her eyes, accentuating the glory and beauty in her. Her physical beauty was still amazing. Even in her fifties, she could catch a man's attention, but the beauty he could see inside was illuminating. He couldn't stand the emotion any longer. "Oh God, Ana!"

He grabbed her face gently and pulled her towards him. With a deep and overflowing flood of emotion, he began to kiss her and with no hint of hesitation, Ana began to return the passion. Their lips embraced in their own dance as their hands began to caress each other with passionate zest.

As the limo pulled up to the steps of Reggie's house, he quickly thanked the driver and led Ana from the car. Despite his aged back, he scooped her up like a bride and carried her into the house, kissing her passionately as they walked.

He kicked the door shut and gently placed her upon the floor in front of the fireplace and with a click of the switch flicked on the flickering glow. With Ana lying aroused on the area rug, Reggie began to undress, turning the radio on to play an endless supply of romantic interludes. Without a moment of hesitation or compunction, Reggie focused his lust upon Ana and zestfully made love to her, over and over again.

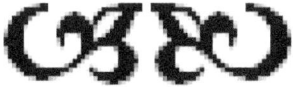

As dawn's first light peeked through the curtains, Ana slowly opened her eyes, hoping that her night hadn't been a dream. Was it real? She could still feel his body on hers and longed to feel him again; then, as she moved slightly in her bed, she felt the warmth of his body next to hers. With awe and wonder, she rolled towards him and smiled. He slept so sweetly that all she wanted to do was get closer to him.

Gently, she moved her hand to his chest and then moved in closer, embracing his scent. He moved slightly and opened his eyes. Without saying a word, he welcomed her head upon his chest and wrapped his arms around her. She lay quietly, listening to his heartbeat as they fell back to sleep for a few more hours.

CHAPTER 23

WITH A WONDERFUL NIGHT BEHIND THEM, Ana got up, showered, and left Reggie to sleep in while she made her way to the kitchen and began to prepare him a hearty breakfast.

Reggie stirred as the buzzing sound of Ana's cell phone began to rumble upon the night table. He groggily reached for it, realizing Ana had gone downstairs. He glanced at the phone window briefly and saw that it was from one of Ana's daughters. Grabbing his robe, he took the phone to her.

As he entered the kitchen, she smiled warmly. "Breakfast is almost ready," she said.

"Great, I'm starved!" he said. He looked at her in her long, pink satin robe with her wet hair pulled up casually and felt a fluttering of pleasure.

Ana became conscious of the stare. "What?" she asked curiously. "I know my hair's still a mess..."

"You're beautiful!" he said.

She smiled softly as she poured the coffee. "Thanks."

"Last night was..."

"I agree."

"I wasn't sure at first, but..."

"I know you're still healing."

"No, not really," he said. "Ruth's gone. I am finally able to let go. Not that my love for her will die, but my heart has made room for more, and, well..."

Ana felt his love as she handed the warm brew.

"Ana...I..." he wanted to say 'I love you,' so desperately, but his nerves were tangled up with his emotions.

"It's okay if you can't say it yet."

"I can. And I do," he affirmed. "Ana, I love you. I know it now, more than ever. Really, I always did love you. That never died, it was just put on hold. Finding you again is nothing short of amazing."

"I felt the..."

"Oh!" he blurted as she began to speak.

"What? What's wrong?"

"I almost forgot. It's your cell."

"Oh," she said as he handed her a buzzing phone. Ana glanced at the screen and saw that it was Emily. "Fifteen messages!?" she gasped.

Reggie felt her fear.

Ana quickly ran through the digits on her phone to begin reviewing her messages. She only made it through the first message, before her heart sank to the floor.

"Mom, you have to call home right away!" Emily pleaded.

"Oh, God," Ana said as her hand began to tremble.

"What is it?" Reggie said as he put down his coffee.

"I don't know," she said. "Emily's panicked." Ana quickly dialed the numbers to her home and waited for Emily to pick up the phone.

Reggie stood by, anxiously hoping to hear that things were alright.

"Mom?" Emily answered.

"Yes Em, it's me. What's up?"

"It's..." suddenly the phone went dead.

"Shit!" Ana screamed. "Battery died. Damn it!"

"Here." Reggie quickly handed her his house phone.

"But the long distance."

"Forget about it. Just call."

She quickly recalled the numbers to her home and waited for the reply.

"Hello?" Emily said.

"Emily? Sorry about that. Phone died. What's-"

"Mom...oh you have to come home!" Emily said as she began to sob.

"Emily, what's wrong?"

"It's..." Emily began to sob and couldn't utter the words. She sounded panicked, and she was struggling to breathe.

"Emily, is it Jack? Is he threatening you?"

Emily didn't reply, but Amy-Lynn interjected and began to speak. "Mom?"

"Amy-Lynn? What's going on? Is Jack threatening-"

"Mom, it's not Jack," Amy-Lynn interrupted. "It's David."

Ana froze. Suddenly her gut wrenched and she could barely feel her legs. As they turned to jelly below her, Reggie quickly grabbed her and moved her body to the chair nearby. Ana's face was white as a sheet.

"What's happened? Is he hurt?" Ana asked.

Amy-Lynn began to weep. "No, Mommy." Ana could hear Amy-Lynn's gulp as she finally uttered the words Ana had always feared. "Mommy, David's dead."

Ana immediately dropped the phone as the blood rushed from her face. The room spun violently as she quickly lost consciousness and began to fall from the chair. Reggie caught her

"Ana!" he gasped.

Amy-Lynn's scream could be heard as Reggie picked up the phone.

"Mommy!" Amy-Lynn cried out.

"Amy-Lynn, it's me, Reggie."

"Where'd Mom go?"

"She's fainted, dear," he said. "Ana. Ana, dear, open your eyes."

"Mom?" Amy-Lynn was terrified.

"Amy-Lynn," he said, trying to sound reassuring. "She'll be fine. What did you tell her?"

"It's my brother David. He died. A bomb or something in Afghanistan." Her tears were flowing full force now and he could hear her sorrow.

"I'm sorry, sweetie; I will bring your mother on the next flight out, okay?"

"Okay." Amy-Lynn hung up the phone and clung to Emily tightly, sobbing desperately.

CHAPTER 24

REGGIE SAT with Ana and brought her back around, dreading the story he'd have to tell her. The details were more than she could bear. The look of pure pain and desperation quickly overshadowed the glow and spark from the night before. She was paralyzed. His heart ached for her; he knew little of what to say. His children were alive and well. He knew the pain of loss but also understood that the pain of losing a child was something few ever got over.

Reggie called Amber and Robert; without hesitation, the two of them arrived at the house and helped make arrangements for a quick departure.

"Ana," Robert said softly, "God be with you." He really didn't know what more to say, but Ana would not cry.

Ana could only nod a 'thank you.' The fear of crying overcame her and she didn't have time to grieve now. She had to get home.

Ana walked around the house in a daze. Her heart had checked out and was already back home with her children; her crushed spirit was soaring the clouds clinging to her son's soul and memory.

Once the car had been packed, Amber and Robert said their compassionate goodbyes and swore they'd make a flight out when the funeral arrangements had been made.

Reggie thanked them as he put Ana into the car and then hugged them goodbye.

"Let us know when you arrive, alright?" Amber asked.

"Of course. The moment I can, I will."

"And take care of her," Robert said. "She's going to need you now."

"I know."

Reggie's kids waved goodbye as the car drove out of sight.

"God be with her," Robert said. "God be with her."

Amber and Robert could only imagine the pain of losing a child, but their compassion went out to Ana and her family.

As the plane began to descend, Ana looked blankly out the window into the night and hoped her children were alright. She hadn't spoken a word during the flight; Reggie allowed her to process her thoughts, offering nothing more than a shoulder or ear, whenever she needed it.

The plane landed smoothly and Reggie led Ana from the plane to the street below, where they quickly hailed a cab to take her home.

When they finally arrived at the apartment, Ana practically leaped from the car before it had even fully stopped. She'd already made it halfway up the stairs before Reggie finished paying the driver and retrieving the bags.

"Must have had to pee, huh?" asked the driver.

"Sure."

"Women," he scoffed with a cynical giggle.

Reggie thanked the driver and waved him on, then turned his attention to the task at hand. She'd locked him out. Not deliberately, he knew that, but he had to buzz upstairs to be let in.

"Hello?"

"Hi. It's me, Reggie."

"You're back?"

"Your mom's on the way up already, but I'm out here with the bags."

"Fine," replied the voice.

"Rachel?" he asked.

"Come on up." She buzzed the door and released it. Her reception was as cold as ice, but he tried to ignore it.

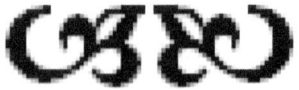

The moment she entered the apartment, Ana was greeted with sorrow from her girls. She'd secretly hoped it was a mistake and that he was simply missing or injured, but then Amy-Lynn showed her the letter of confirmation.

The 'regret to inform' gripped her soul like a bear trap, crushing it into pieces. Her body ached so desperately and she was so tired, but when she looked at her girls she saw how much they needed her.

As she spoke, Reggie prodded his way inside.

"It says he was a hero," she explained to them. "And they'll be bringing his body home to us tomorrow." She struggled with the tears and emotion but chose to be strong for her daughters.

"What can we do, Mom?" Emily asked.

"Have you called his friends?"

"Some of them."

"Call as many as you can, let them know what's happened and that we will be notifying them of the funeral date and time once the military has organized it. And what about Carl? Has he been by at all?"

The girls shook their heads.

"He knows, doesn't he?"

"Yes, Mom. When they couldn't find you, they told him. That's how I found out," said Rachel. "Then I called Em."

"That son of a-!" she wanted to cuss him out, but would not in front of the girls. She turned around quickly and looked Reggie in the eye. "How could he take this so cold-ly?" she asked.

Reggie was speechless, but his instinct was to go to Carl's place and beat the fucking shit out of the loser.

"This is our son!" Ana continued. "It's one thing to disown me, but David was his son. And these girls need their dad!"

"I agree," Reggie said. "Is there anything I can do?"

"I can't say what I want right now," Ana said. "I'm far too emotional."

Only a night ago, she and Reggie had made passionate

love and had begun a new life together. Now that seemed like a lifetime ago. In a blink, her life had changed forever.

"Girls, we have arrangements to make for your brother's memorial. Let's put on a pot of tea and start finding some pictures and things for a commemorative movie to play for everyone, ok?"

Reggie took the bags to Ana's room and then sat quietly as he listened to the women talk about David and his many amazing stories.

David had lived an exemplary life. Each detail showed his strong character and charm. A good-looking young man, struck down in his prime, saving young children from a roadside bomb.

CHAPTER 25

CARL BARELY SHOWED an interest in the death of their son. He made an appearance — for argument's sake — but showed little to no emotion. Reggie stood by the family every step of the way. It's what Ana would have done for him. It's what Ana did do for him, and he could do nothing less than offer the support she needed.

A row of mourners sobbed desperately as soldiers in full dress carried his casket passed. War had brought fear to the country and David took a stand against the attack for the sake of peace. Although he never agreed with the war, he'd hoped that by working with the people, he could teach them a better way. A way toward peace and freedom. Freedom was a gift granted by his forefathers and he chose to do the same for the next generation.

When the flag was folded and the gun salute echoed through the hills, the tears Ana had bottled up began to pour. Reggie knew it would happen when she was ready, but the combination of the music and the Purple Heart she clung to sent her emotions plummeting out of control.

Reggie embraced Ana and let her sob as long as she needed. Carl watched jealously. Rachel was not impressed.

"Really, Reggie?" she scoffed. "You choose now to rub your hands all over my mother? This is my brother's funeral, not your love-making paradise."

Reggie was shocked, but Ana was enraged.

"Rachel! How dare you speak to Reggie like that? He's done nothing but support and respect us through this terrible time."

"Yeah, so he can get in your pants!"

Ana, with surged emotion, slapped Rachel across the face. "How dare you speak to me that way!"

"I think it's your fault daddy fucked around!"

"Watch your mouth!" Ana said. "This is David's funeral. I will not have you shit on his memory, do you hear me?"

"Sure, bitch!"

"Don't talk to your mother like that!" Reggie said.

"I'll handle this!" Ana scoffed.

Reggie pulled back. He hadn't meant to get involved, but his children wouldn't have been allowed to speak to Ruth that way, nor would he expect that of Ana's children. "Sorry, Ana," he said. "I didn't mean."

Rachel interrupted. "Why don't you let my mother be and go back east where you belong?!"

"Rachel, stop!" Emily said.

"Honestly Rachel, I don't mean any harm here. I know you're in pain."

"You don't know shit!" Rachel screamed again. "You think that just because your wife died that you can simply move into our lives as your replacement? I'm sure you can find someone local!"

"Rachel, stop!" Ana said.

"No! It's me or him. I won't have him in my life. You choose! Choose now or I'm gone!"

"Why are you doing this?" Amy-Lynn asked.

"He's trying to replace Daddy and I'm not going to let it happen. Daddy will stop his craziness and when he does, things will be like they used to be."

"They can't be Rachel," Ana said.

"You'll try! You have to!"

"Rachel."

"I mean it, Mother. It's me or him!"

"Rachel, let's go home and talk this over. Alright? Try and calm down," Ana said.

"I'm not going if he's going."

Reggie felt sick. Why did this girl hate him so much? Emily and Amy-Lynn were fine, but Rachel's defiance put them in an awkward position.

Ana looked at Reggie, realizing that Rachel needed her attention. "Reggie, I'm sorry, but I'm not going to be able to see you for a while."

"Come on Ana, she'll be fine. She's just upset," Reggie suggested.

"Mommy, you can't bring him to the house. He touched me!"

"What do you mean, he touched you?"

Reggie looked at her in horror. "I did what?"

"You tried to fuck me, you old fart!"

"I did no such thing!" he replied.

"He did it! One of the days you were at work, he came by. He tried to fuck me!"

"Reggie!?" Ana turned and looked at him coldly. "Did you touch my daughter?"

"That's not true!" Amy-Lynn snapped. "He wouldn't do that!"

"Stay out of this, Amy-Lynn!" Rachel screamed. "He didn't touch you because you're too skinny. He likes breasts. Like these! Don't you, you old pervert!"

"Oh my God!" Reggie replied. "I don't believe what I'm hearing!"

"I swear, Reggie." Ana began to stare him down.

"Ana, I didn't do this!"

"Get out!" she screamed. "I will mail you your shit, but you are not coming home with me! You're lucky I'm letting you walk!"

"He likes young girls, Mommy."

"I should have known better than to trust you!" Ana screamed.

"Ana, I swear!"

"Just go! Go while I still have my temper in check," Ana scorned.

"But Ana, I love you!"

"Don't say that again!"

"I..." Reggie looked at Ana's face and could not find the words to rebuke these allegations. "I'll go." He looked at Rachel with a look of disappointment. He knew she was hurting, but how this had come about was beyond his understanding. His heart was shattered and he was power-less to do anything as long as Ana's emotions and Rachel's disdain were so elevated.

CHAPTER 26

REGGIE RODE on the plane back to Philadelphia, leaving behind his belongings and his heart. Ana had believed Rachel. Why wouldn't she? But it killed him to think she'd simply discarded him. So much love had been shared only a few days earlier and now his heart was torn for the second time in a year.

As he entered the house, he was surprised to find Amber there. "Dad?" she asked. "I wasn't expecting you back for a few more days. I just came by to-" She saw the look of pain and sorrow clouding his eyes. "Daddy, what is it?"

"It's Ana," he muttered.

"What happened?"

"We're over."

"What? How?"

"Her daughter, Rachel, decided to kick up a fuss and then accused me of molesting her."

"What the fuck?" Amber groaned. "As if!"

"Ana wouldn't hear me after that."

"Oh, Daddy!" Amber felt her heartbreaking. "I'm so, so sorry!"

"I'm just going to go to bed," he mumbled. "You're okay down here, right?"

"Sure."

Amber was reluctant to leave him, but her children were waiting at home and Gary was working the night shift. She couldn't stay, but her heart longed to be with her dad at the moment.

Reggie dragged his feet up the stairs and then down the hall to his room. As he entered he saw the pink robe Ana had left behind and his heart began to break. He heard a car door close and the engine rev and he figured the coast was clear. Amber was heading home and now he had a chance to cry.

Like a child in despair, he clung to the robe and sobbed and sobbed and sobbed.

Grabbing a picture of Ana from his nightstand, he cried more. "I can't believe I lost you again."

With an urge to drink away the pain, he wandered downstairs to the liquor cabinet and poured himself a glass of Scotch. It went down warm and smooth, but it did not mask the pain.

Again, he poured himself a shot, but it did not numb the pain. Finally, burdened with grief, he began to chug the bottle like a bottle of Sprite, chasing the pain as far down as he could.

His head began to spin and his heart began to pound, but he could still feel the pain.

"Why did you do this, Ana!?" he shouted. "Why? I loved you. I always loved you!"

He took the empty bottle of Scotch and chucked it

across the room, shattering his wedding day photo. "Oh fuck!" he cried. "What did I do?"

Unsatisfied, he next grabbed a bottle of brandy. The bottle was nearly empty before he started drinking, so it didn't take long for him to finish it off.

Staggered and drunk, he stumbled out the door and fumbled for his car keys, but drunk as he was, he couldn't find them. In a rage he kicked the car door, denting it.

With a 24-hour Kroger's less than two blocks away, he began to make his way to the store for the next fix. His mind was a blur of thoughts and emotions, but he wanted the voices to stop. His father had been a drunk his entire adult life and lacked little character as a result of it. Reggie swore never to let it get this far, but tonight he didn't give a rat's ass. He was going to chase that pain away.

He wandered into the store and began to walk the aisles with his cart, picking up various bottles of liquor. As he walked along, a woman from the neighborhood recognized him.

"Hi, Reggie," she greeted. "What are you doing here?"

"Nottin'," he stammered.

He swaggered as he stood and his eyes were bright red. She recognized the symptoms. "Are you drunk?" she asked. "I don't think I've ever seen you drunk."

"I'm fine. Just in need of some stuff," he said through slurred words.

"I don't think you're going to find relief this way," she cautioned. "Let me drive you home."

"No!" he blurted. "I'm fine. I will pay for my stuff and I'll get my own home self, thank you very much."

The woman was shocked. This was not like him at all. "Reggie, please, what can I do?"

"Just leave me alone, Kathy."

"It's Kelly. And I don't know if I can do that."

"For fuck sakes, I'm allowed to have a drink now and then without you getting involved, aren't I?"

Kelly tried to reason with him, but his desperation and anger were only amplified by the alcohol. The only thing she could do was watch from afar and follow him, hoping to keep him from harm.

She began to scroll through her cell numbers to find Amber's number. "Damn. I don't have it," she mumbled.

After gathering an assortment of bottles, Reggie proceeded to the checkout and paid, but the manager was concerned and interjected.

"Sir, are you driving?"

"No, fool, I couldn't find the keys."

"Thank God!" he said. "Can I call you a cab?"

"I'm fine. Why can't you just leave me alone? Huh?"

Reggie was fed up with people 'getting in his face,' even if their concern was merited.

As he staggered from the store with his hands full of liquor, he began walking up the street toward his house. Kelly followed slowly in her car. Reggie paused to open the bottle of rum and began guzzling it as fast he could. The world spun crazily around him as he came into view of his home, but he was barely able to focus on the steps he needed to take. He stepped into the road without noticing the motorist zooming toward him in the oncoming lane.

In an instant, Reggie's body was struck and the bottles of liquor flew every which way. Kelly screamed in her car, swerving to miss his body as it tumbled helplessly over the hood of the car and then finally landed hard on the ground in front of her. She slammed the brakes, coming within inches of his broken body.

The other driver never even stopped.

"Fucking loser!" Kelly yelled. Then, turning her attention back to Reggie, she said, "Reggie? Reggie, can you hear me?" She touched his body gently, but he did not respond. Reggie's neighbor had heard the commotion and ran to the scene to investigate.

"What happened here?"

"The driver-," she said pointing down the street, "-hit him."

At first he didn't know who 'he' was, but as he began to dial 911, he realized the dreaded truth, "Oh shit! It's Reggie!"

"Do you know first aid?" Kelly asked.

"Yes. Do you?"

"No."

Kelly took the phone and spoke to the operator while the neighbor began to review Reggie's injuries. The look on his face was not hopeful.

"Ambulance is on its way," she said.

"Great. Now go into his house and find his kids' numbers."

CHAPTER 27

ANA SAT IN HER ROOM, sulking. She missed Reggie's touch. She missed his smell. She felt enraged and guilty that she'd allowed this man to get close to her only to learn he'd been making a play for her daughter. Nothing made sense. Her heart ached.

Restless, she stepped out upon the balcony and stared blankly over the sunset water. The bellowing sounds of whales echoed through the neighborhood; it hurt to hear that sound. How she wished she was embracing Reggie right now.

"Stop it, Ana!" she said to herself. "You can't be in love with him still. I should hate him. I do hate him!" The agony was overwhelming.

Emily and Amy-Lynn sat in the living room watching "Mama Mia" for the 400th time, while Rachel finished combing her freshly washed hair. She felt guilty, but she'd gotten rid of him. She should have felt glad, but her act hadn't fixed the problem with her parents. Instead, Carl moved in with yet another woman, who was the same age as his daughter, Emily. Disgraceful. He'd been ignoring the girls' phone calls and it hurt.

Rachel stepped out of the bathroom and suddenly heard a stirring down the hall. She peeked into Cayson's room and saw that he was sound asleep, so she left him alone. Then she heard the sounds of crying coming from her mother's room.

The door was open just a touch so she peeked in undetected. Her mother was sitting on the balcony, sobbing softly — trying not to be heard. Rachel stepped in quietly and tried to approach, to listen closer.

The glistening sunset danced upon Ana's blonde hair and highlighted the moisture upon her face. She had been crying. Rachel hoped it was from missing David and was about to join her mother when she heard her mother talking to herself.

"Oh, Reggie," she sniffed, looking at the photos on her phone. "Why did you have to mess this up? I loved you! Damn it. I loved you. How could you hurt my daughter? I thought you loved me, too. You wouldn't have done it if you loved me. Damn it, Reggie! Damn you!"

Rachel felt sick to her stomach. She'd hurt her mother and told a terrible lie. Her deception destroyed Ana's chance for love and happiness. Rachel had hoped for Carl's repentance, but now she realized his devotion to his family was nonexistent. His love and devotion to Ana was gone and now she was alone and hurt.

"What have I done?" she asked herself as tears fell from her face.

Amy-Lynn, who was walking by the room, also heard her mother's sobs. She saw the open door and looked inside the room. Seeing Rachel standing in the middle of the room, Amy-Lynn blurted out, "Are you spying?"

Rachel jumped.

Ana heard them both.

"Rachel? Amy-Lynn? What are you doing there? Are you spying on me?" Ana asked.

"No mother," Amy-Lynn replied. "I just came in when I saw the door open and heard you crying. I was surprised to find Rachel in here."

"How long have you been standing there Rachel?"

"I don't know," she replied awkwardly.

"I don't like you spying on me," Ana scolded. "I needed a moment to myself. Is that too much to ask?"

"I'm sorry," Rachel said.

"You miss David, Mom?" Amy-Lynn asked.

"Yes," Ana said. "Of course I miss him. I always will. He was my son."

"But that's not why you were crying, is it?" Emily said as she walked in to join the party.

"What do you mean?"

"It's Reggie, isn't it?" Emily asked.

"Reggie's done and over with. He's no good. I can't be in love with a man who molests my daughter," Ana said. "I'll be fine. As long as my girls are safe."

"I didn't see that in him," Amy-Lynn confessed. "He seemed like such a great man."

"I know," Ana said. She wanted to cry again but held it back.

"I didn't get to know him long," Emily said. "But I thought he was a good man, too. You seemed so happy together."

Ana's lip began to quiver again. "Girls, I need to be alone right now, okay?"

"Mom?" Rachel mumbled. "I need to tell you something."

"Not now, Rachel. I'm sorry, but I need a few moments."

"But, I..."

"Come on, Rachel," Emily directed. "Let's give Mom a break."

The three girls left the room and wandered into the kitchen. Emily put on a pot of tea and the three girls sat at the bar table and waited for the water to steep.

"I can't believe he did that to you, Rachel," Emily said. "I wish I'd known sooner. I would have stopped him before he hurt you. This whole thing is killing Mom!"

"I know. She really loved him," said Amy-Lynn.

"What did he do to you anyways?" Emily asked.

"What do you mean?" Rachel asked.

"How did he 'touch you'?" Emily asked. "I don't mean to drag up the details, but honestly we should have him charged."

"Oh no!" Rachel replied. "You can't do that!"

"Why not?" Amy-Lynn asked. "He used Mom to get you alone. That's a crime!"

"He didn't," Rachel blurted without thinking.

"Didn't what?" Emily asked.

"No, it's nothing. I just don't want to talk about it," said Rachel.

"Rachel?" Emily asked. "He did do those things, right?"

Rachel wanted to defend herself, but the guilt was eating her up inside.

"I..." She tucked her lips tightly as her eyes began to fill with tears. "I didn't mean to."

"Didn't mean to what?" Ana asked, walking into the kitchen.

"Oh, Mommy." Rachel's guilt burst wide open and she began to sob uncontrollably.

"Oh, sweetie. I'm sorry he hurt you. If I had known he was capable..."

"He wasn't."

"He wasn't what?" Ana asked, pulling Rachel back to face her directly.

"I feel terrible. I don't even know why I said it. I'm sorry."

"Sorry for what?" Ana asked, becoming more intense. "You didn't make it up, did you?"

Rachel's face froze as she looked at Ana. She couldn't find the words to speak, but she slowly nodded her head.

"You did?" Emily asked. "You made it up?"

Rachel's eyes overflowed with tears in response.

"You lied about Reggie?!" Amy-Lynn scolded.

Ana's mouth opened wide and her eyes filled with tears. "I cannot believe you did this to me! You accused a perfectly good man of molestation, just to get rid of him? Do you loathe me that much?"

"I don't loathe you. I just want Daddy back."

"I don't want Daddy back!" Ana blurted out. "Did you ever think of that?"

"I just thought..."

"Well, you thought wrong!"

"I'm sorry!"

"Mommy," Amy-Lynn interrupted. "You need to call him."

"I will. Rachel, I..." Ana was furious. A flurry of accusations was on the tip of her tongue, but out of love for her child, she held back. "I will talk to you more about this when I'm not so angry."

"I'm sorry, Mom."

"I know you are, but sometimes sorry just isn't enough. I

love you, but I have lost a man who loves me. I only hope I can get his forgiveness now."

Ana immediately retreated to her room.

CHAPTER 28

IT WAS touch and go at the hospital. Reggie's body was terribly broken. The emergency room specialists worked feverishly to stabilize him as they rushed him to the operating room.

The neighbor and Kelly waited impatiently for Amber, William, and Robert to arrive. Nora had agreed to stay with the children while the others rushed to their father's side.

"Robert," said the neighbor.

"Mr. Rickman," he replied, shaking her hand. "What happened, do you know?"

"I saw the whole thing!" Kelly said. "My name is Kelly. I was friends with your mother."

"I recognize you from the funeral," William said.

"Yes," she replied. "I was there."

"You saw the whole thing?" Amber asked. "What happened?"

Kelly looked uncomfortable and pale, "I, well, he was hit by a car."

"At two in the morning?" William said. "Dad doesn't go outside at that hour. He's usually in bed."

"I knew I should have stayed with him," Amber said. "He was so distraught."

"About what?" William asked.

"I didn't get a chance to tell you, but it seems Ana's daughter accused him of inappropriate behavior, and, well...Ana kicked him out."

"Without giving him the benefit of the doubt?"

"There's no way in hell Dad would hurt a child!"

"I know that."

"We all know that," said Kelly. "I had no idea what was bothering him when I saw him at the store."

"What store?"

Kelly sighed. "He was down the street at Kroger. I saw him staggering."

"Drunk?" Amber asked.

"Dad doesn't get drunk!" William said.

"I guess he was hurting pretty badly then," Kelly said.

"How drunk?" Robert asked.

"One to ten? I'd say an eleven."

"What was he doing at Kroger?"

"Buying more booze," Kelly replied. "Most of it got smashed when the car." She gulped as she shuttered.

Amber was about to burst into tears when the physician entered the waiting room.

"Are you Reginald's family?" he asked.

"Yes," Robert replied, taking charge. "We're his kids."

"Is he okay?" Amber blurted. "Can we go see him?"

"You need to sit down," said the doctor.

"Oh, God!" Amber freaked, "Is he...?"

"He is alive, but his injuries are critical," the doctor explained. "He has multiple fractures. We had to remove the spleen, his liver is enlarged, his sternum and three ribs were broken, which ruptured his left lung, and he has bleeding in the brain. That's not to mention the broken leg and arm."

"Oh, God!"

"Is he going to be okay?" William asked.

"The next few days will determine that. His injuries are severe. It could go either way."

"Can we sit with him?" Amber asked.

"You should know, he's in a coma."

"A coma!" Amber gasped as she burst into tears and buried her face in Gary's arms. He comforted her, while the two boys stood coldly in disbelief.

"We can't lose him!" William said. "We haven't gotten over our mother's death, and now this?"

"This is unbelievable," Gary said.

"Should we call Ana?" Robert suggested.

"No!" Amber blurted. "I don't want her near my father! This is her fault!"

"I know there's been a mix-up here, but I'm sure she'd like to know," Robert said.

"No, Robert, not now! Please!"

Robert was reluctant but agreed.

The three kids entered the room to sit with Reggie. They were immediately gripped with unbelievable shock at the sight of their father's body. He was pale, bruised, swollen, and still. Multiple machines beeped and hissed as they worked together to maintain his life.

Amber suddenly felt ill and rushed to a nearby garbage can where she vomited several times. Her grief sent her to the floor and her husband comforted her as best he could. As she stood up and turned to look back at Reggie, the shock and horror of the moment overtook her and her face went white as a sheet. Her legs gave way and she collapsed like a ragdoll. Gary caught her before she hit the floor, but Amber was out cold.

The medical staff immediately removed her from the room and moved her to another location to recover.

While she was being attended to, Robert and William worried about Reggie's situation.

"This cannot be happening," Robert whispered.

"Do you think we should call Ana?" William asked.

"Maybe, but the way Amber's handling this, I don't know if I want to just yet."

CHAPTER 29

ANA PICKED up the phone and quickly dialed Reggie's home number. The answering machine picked up; Ana was disappointed but chose to leave him a message.

"Hi, Reggie," she said softly, "It's me, Ana. Please call me. I'm sorry. I just want to talk to you. Please call."

She hung up the phone and paced the floor anxiously until fatigue took over and she finally was exhausted enough to sleep.

The next day at work, she texted him, emailed him and called his house several times. Message after message, she hoped he would hear her sincerity and forgive her. He had to call her back, he just had to.

With no reply, her heart continued to ache. Somehow, he had to find it in him to forgive her.

"Reggie, I love you. I miss you. Please, let's talk?"

Ana even called Reggie's workplace, but the only reply she got — on Amber's say-so — was that Reggie was not able to take her call. Her heart broke, over and over again.

Then, finally, after four days of begging and pleading she came to the conclusion that he just didn't want to talk to her, and probably never would. She hated that it hurt so much.

Rachel felt the ache in her mother's heart and hated that she'd been the one to cause it. Although Ana had forgiven Rachel's malicious attack, the lie had put a rift between them and it was hard to recover that trust.

Wanting to make things right, Rachel tried to reconnect with Ana.

She found Reggie's office number and dialed it.

"Reggie Whitaker's Office" replied the secretary.

"Hello, may I please speak with Mr. Whitaker?" Rachel asked, trying to sound grown up and official.

"May I ask who is calling?"

"My name is Mrs. Tracy. I need his services," she replied.

"Well, Mrs. Tracy, I'm afraid you won't be able to talk to him at this time."

"Why not?" Rachel replied.

"Well ma'am, if you're not from around here you must not know."

"Know what?"

"Reggie's been in the hospital for the past week."

"Hospital?" Rachel gasped. "What happened?"

"Well, I'm not able to give you details, ma'am, but he is in critical condition."

"Holy shit!" Rachel said.

Rachel quickly hung up the phone and began to review the news reports in the area about Reggie's accident. She was able to quickly piece together the story with a quick Google search.

She felt sick to her stomach, but she knew what she had to do.

She had Emily join her in telling Ana. Amy-Lynn was at school.

Entering Ana's office, the two girls got Kat's permission to enter the office, where Ana was working hard on a project.

"Hi, Mom?" Emily said, opening the door slowly.

"Emily?" Ana replied. "What are you doing here?"

Rachel poked her head in.

"What are you girl's doing here? Where's Cayson?"

"I left him with the sitter."

"Okay, so is everything okay?" Ana asked. The look on the girls' faces did not indicate a 'happy to see you' visit.

"It's about Reggie," Rachel said.

"Rachel, I already forgave you. Besides, he's moved on."

Emily shook her head. "Mom, listen to us."

Ana's gut began to churn. "What's going on?"

"I called his office," Rachel said.

"What? Why?"

"I wanted to plead with him to give you another chance. I wanted to apologize."

"He ignored your call?"

"No, not exactly."

"What then?"

"I spoke with the secretary and found out."

"Found out what?"

"Reggie's in the hospital."

"What?" Ana felt sick. "What happened?"

"They didn't tell me much on the phone, but apparently it made the news there. So I looked it up."

"Just tell me, Rachel."

"He's in bad shape, Mom."

Ana's eyes began to fill with tears. "How bad?"

"He's in a coma."

"A coma!"

Rachel quickly filled Ana in on the details of the accident and then Ana called the hospital for information. The hospital would not disclose any information and Amber would not accept any calls.

"I'm going to him!" Ana said.

Without another thought, Ana quickly put together her things, kissed her girls goodbye, and caught the next plane to Pennsylvania. Her heart ached the whole time as she longed to see him again.

"Reggie, don't leave me now. I'm coming to you! I'm coming!"

CHAPTER 30

ANA'S FLIGHT felt long and grueling. She tried to relax, but anxiety and uncertainty overshadowed all reason. The only thing on her mind was the man with silvery-speckled hair who had stolen her heart so long ago.

Ana quickly dropped her things off at a local motel and then took a cab to the hospital. She continued trying to contact Amber, but she never got an answer; Ana knew she'd have to do some explaining. Nonetheless, she was determined to see him again.

When she finally reached the hospital, she immediately located Reggie's unit and spoke to the nurses at the station. "Reggie Whitaker's room please," she said boldly.

"Are you family?"

"No, but I do love him."

"Oh. You're the one," said the nurse sternly. "Wait here."

The nurse walked off with disdain and entered a room to the left. Ana followed quietly, peeked into the room, and could only see the foot of the bed. She heard talking, but the soft whispers were too muffled to understand.

Soon after, Robert exited the room.

"You came," Robert said.

"Of course, I came," she replied. "You should have called me."

"I wanted to, but..."

"You left my dad," William said, joining the conversation. "Why would we call you?"

"Because I love him!"

"He loved you, too, and that's why he's here now!"

"I don't know anything about the accident."

"Accident?" William replied. "He was so crushed by what happened in California that he drank himself into a stupor and staggered in front of a speeding car. That's what happened."

Ana's eyes welled with tears. "Oh God!" she sobbed. "I'm sorry. God, I know it was stupid for me to think that there was any truth to the allegations. I just...oh, God..."

"It was my fault!" said another voice.

They all turned around to see Rachel.

"I'm Rachel," she said, trembling and awkward.

"You accused my dad of molesting you and now you're here to do what? Watch him die?" William asked.

Rachel began to sob. "No...no, I'm sorry. This wasn't my mother's fault. She only believed me. My brother had just died. She believed me because she loves me. She didn't want to believe it. She wanted to protect me. She loves him. I know that now. I know she was happier with him than with anyone ever in her life. And I think he loved her just as much."

"You really hurt a good man," Robert said.

"I know. I was stupid. I don't care if you all hate me, but don't punish my mom. She needs him and I think he needs her, too."

Robert and William recognized her sincerity and agreed.

"Alright," Robert said. "Ana, you can see him. But if for any moment I think you are jeopardizing his health, I will ask you to leave. Got it?"

"I understand. I only want to see him well again."

"Fine," Robert said. "Come with me. Rachel, we'll talk soon."

Rachel nodded and accepted that she would need to explain herself more, but at least now her mother would be able to see Reggie.

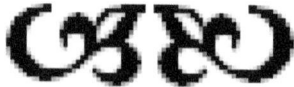

As she stepped into the hospital room, Ana got her first look at Reggie's broken body. Her eyes were swollen, his arm was resting in a support, his leg was elevated, and there were tubes and leads tied to various parts of his body. He was still and pale. Her heart sank.

"Oh, God," she whispered. Tears welled up in her eyes as she looked at him and all the images of their time together came rushing back in a jangled sequence.

She found an empty chair and sat down quietly beside him. Then she gently took one of his hands in her own and held it to her lips. Gently she kissed it as a tear ran down her face.

"Oh, my Reggie," she sniffed. "I am so, so sorry! I know

you didn't do those things and I should have believed you from the start. Oh, God. I lost you once... I don't want to lose you again."

As she sat with him, Amber entered the room. At first, she wanted to scream, but with Ana's back to her, Robert urged her quietly to just listen.

"Reggie," she said again, stroking his cheek. "Please come back to us. I love you. Your kids are here. And those beautiful grandbabies need their grandpa. Please come back... Open your eyes.

"I love you! I've loved you since the day we met and I never stopped. I love you more than ever and I need you. God. I'm sorry. Please, forgive me. I love you!" Tears streamed down her face and her sincerity touched Amber's heart.

Approaching Ana quietly, Amber placed a hand on her shoulder.

Ana turned and looked Amber in the eyes.

"Oh God, Amber... I'm so, so sorry!" Ana stood up, still holding Reggie's hand. "I know you don't want me here. I understand why."

"Quiet, Ana." Amber interrupted. "Just, stop."

Ana trembled and wanted to crawl into a corner. She tried to brace herself for whatever Amber was going to say.

"Ana. Thank you for coming."

Ana looked shocked.

"I was mad and, yes, I blamed you for this," Amber said, choking on her tears. "But I recognize true love and I know you love my dad the way he loves you."

"I do."

"You belong here, Ana."

"Amber, thank you!"

The two women embraced and sobbed quietly together until the healing had begun.

"You need to be here. I will take Rachel. We'll get your things at the motel. You will stay with us, alright?"

Ana nodded. "Thank you."

"I know this has been a rollercoaster for all of us. My only focus right now is my dad."

"Mine, too."

"I know it is. Keep talking to him. Let him know you're here."

CHAPTER 31

ANA SAT with Reggie for the next week, never leaving his side. She slept in the chair and ate the food Rachel brought for her. She didn't give up. Not once.

"Do you remember the day we met? Not at the school, but in Santa Monica? I was so amazed to see you again. You took my breath away. I didn't tell you then, but immediately, I thought it was fate. Our love was meant to be."

"Do you remember the delicious meal at Melisse? Wow! That place was something! But you made it extraordinary."

"I wanted to tell you the last time we were together just how much I loved you, but I couldn't. I didn't want to scare you, but every time I saw you smile, when I saw you dance with your daughter and granddaughters at William's wedding, when I heard you tell how proud you were at William's wedding, when I saw you play Monopoly with Amy-Lynn, and when I saw your face under the moonlight in Santa Monica...each and every moment you took my breath away. All I wanted to do was hold you and touch you.

"All I want to do now is plan on making you happy the

rest of your days. I can't tell you enough how much I love you, Reginald Whitaker!"

She held his hand, touched his face, and ran her fingers through his hair every chance she got, hoping for some kind of response.

Then, one evening, after telling him a story about their night together in bed, she kissed his chest gently, then placed her head on the side of the bed and moved her fingers along his leg softly. "I love you, Reggie."

A tear ran from her face as her fatigue began to overwhelm her when suddenly she felt a flicker upon her head. She opened her eyes and thought for a moment that she had found herself in a dream.

The machines' beeping seemed to increase slightly. She felt the flutter again.

She sat up and looked at Reggie's hand. It was still, but she was curious. "Reggie, did you move your hand?" she asked.

The moment was silent.

"Reggie, if you can hear me, can you move your fingers again?"

She stared at the fingers, but it seemed as though there would be no response. Then suddenly they moved. She did a double take. And again, they moved.

She looked up at his face and saw that the lids of his eyes were flickering. Her heart skipped a beat as she stood up and looked at him directly. "Oh God!" she kissed his face. "I'll be right back!"

Ana ran out to the nurses' station and demanded their attention. The team entered the room, with the doctor immediately following behind them.

"I swear, he moved his fingers! Then I saw his lids flickering."

The doctor grabbed his light and pried Reggie's eyes open, shining the light into his pupils. With a start, Reggie flinched and blinked quickly.

"Oh, God! Did you see that?" Ana cried.

"Reggie? This is Doctor Clark. Can you open your eyes for me?" he asked.

At first, there was no response, but Ana wasn't patient. "Reggie, it's me, Ana. Can you please open your gorgeous blue eyes?"

With a little struggle, Reggie finally opened his eyes and began to groggily scan the room. His gaze settled on Ana. With a little effort, he smiled at her as a tear rolled down his cheek.

Ana's eyes were full of tears and her heart leaped. "Welcome back, baby! Welcome back!" The joy in her heart was mountainous and overpowering. The fire of love was in full blaze and she wasn't about to let it be doused by anything.

Once the doctor had finished his examination, Ana was left to sit with Reggie once again. A mask was fastened to his face, providing oxygen, but many of the tubes had been removed.

With a raspy, fatigued throat he attempted to speak. "I love you, Ana," he whispered.

"I love you, too!" she said.

She leaned down and kissed his lips tenderly.

He used all his strength to raise his arm and place it around her gently. As she embraced him, Amber walked into the room with eyes of wonder.

"Daddy!" she gasped.

Ana stood up and moved to the side so Reggie could embrace his children as they arrived one at a time.

Reggie was pleased to receive so much love.

Finally, after everyone had had their moment of celebration, Rachel hesitantly entered the room. She gulped nervously.

"Reggie?" she said softly.

He looked at her with deep concern.

"I'm so sorry…"

Reggie smiled warmly. "I understand." His voice was warm and sincere. Then he gestured her to move closer to the bed. "I want you to know, I love your mother."

"I know that."

"I'm glad. And if given the chance, I'd love to get to know you better too."

"I'd like that, too, Reggie."

She carefully hugged the man. Ana watched fondly as two of the people she loved most in this world finally began to bond.

CHAPTER 32

REGGIE SPENT the next several months recovering in the hospital and the family stayed nearby and encouraged his recovery faithfully. Rachel remained with Reggie, bonding with him daily, while Ana returned to California for a short time to complete some business.

Finally, Reggie was deemed healthy enough to be released from the hospital. Ana made arrangements with her company to do some work from Pennsylvania while she helped care for Reggie at home.

Amy-Lynn, Emily, and little Cayson decided to make the trip with their mother to spend some time getting to know the man who'd won Ana's heart. Chester joined them on the flight, complaining adamantly for the entire trip.

Arriving in Pennsylvania, Ana set the girls up at the house with Cayson and Chester and then proceeded to the hospital to pick Reggie up. She hadn't seen him in almost a week and was anxious to see him once again.

As she entered the hospital, she made her way to the room he'd been in, but the bed was made and empty. The patient in the next bed was sound asleep, so she went to the nurses' station. She exited the room and began walking toward the desk when she heard a familiar voice.

"Ana?"

She immediately turned around and her eyes popped open wide. There, at the end of the hallway, stood Reggie. Using a cane, he began to walk toward her.

"Oh my God!" she cried. "You're walking!"

"Only for the past few days," he said. "Sea legs are still a little rubbery, but they're coming along."

"I'm thrilled!"

"I'm so happy to see you!" he said.

"I missed you," Ana said.

The nurse who'd been walking with Reggie stepped back to give them a moment of privacy.

"God, you look beautiful!" he said.

"Oh no, I'm a mess," she said. A long flight with an irritable cat had left her a little disheveled, but that's not what Reggie saw. Not allowing her to say another word, Reggie dropped his cane, grabbed her face, pulled her close, and with no hesitation the two embraced in an intensively passionate kiss.

The hospital room soon became a romantic dance floor as the two of them began to sway back and forth. Although Reggie's leg was wobbly and his body was not yet fully healed, he was deeply focused on Ana. All other worries and woes simply disappeared.

Ana's heart melted as he began to kiss her neck gently and his fingers ran through her hair. She wanted him so badly, but the nurses' station was not the ideal place; still, for the moment, their passion overshadowed all realistic details.

Finally, after an intense emotional experience, Ana whispered, "Let's get you home, shall we?"

He leaned back and smiled brightly at her. "Yes, let's go home."

With a few signatures and the doctor's green light, Ana gently wheeled Reggie to the parking lot, loaded him into the car, and helped him buckle up. He was now free of his casts, and for the most part he was mending well. As she leaned over to assist him with the seat belt Reggie grabbed her again and pulled her lips to his.

"God, it feels good to touch you again!"

The two of them began to kiss so intensely, they forgot there were people waiting to load and unload. Reggie's hands, though still a little bruised, enjoyed caressing her body while his lips wrapped around her tongue. She desperately wanted to make love to him and returned his affection with a tongue slip. She gently caressed his chest and moaned as he touched her breast passionately. They would have done much more, but the annoyed patients behind them had lost their patience and began to honk the horn. They almost hadn't noticed until the security guard interrupted them.

"You folks need a room or something?" he asked.

Ana jolted. "Oh, God, I'm sorry." she said.

The guard nodded with a sinister smile. "It's fine. You kids get going now. Take your hormones home, alright?" He winked as he stepped back from the car.

Ana smiled and Reggie grinned like a high school boy. "Thanks, man," he said.

Ana got into the car and began to drive back to Reggie's house. Her heart pounded, thrilled that she and Reggie were being given yet another chance together.

Reggie's eyes were locked on her for the entire ride; he gently rubbed her thigh as she drove.

CHAPTER 33

THE GIRLS HAD DECIDED to take advantage of their time alone in Reggie's home and quickly put together a fantastically romantic evening. Reggie, who'd discussed his thoughts with Rachel earlier in the week, gained her permission to move forward in the relationship with Ana.

Reggie made the financial arrangements for Rachel to visit a local jeweler where she was to pick out the perfect ring.

The meal consisted of all of their mom's favorites, as directed by Reggie. William's wife, Faith, helped Amy-Lynn and Rachel cook the most delectable morsels for the six-course dinner.

While the chefs were busy in the kitchen with the food preparations, Emily began to create the atmosphere. She filled the room with long-stem candles and white orchids — Ana's favorite flower. Then she set up the stereo to play an endless list of the most romantic music she could create with her MP3 collection. Then she moved the table against the wall of the room, making a space for dancing. Then, with the music and candles ready, she started work on the table.

She began with a white linen cloth draped carefully over the table. Then she removed all of the chairs, save two. She placed two candles and a beautiful centerpiece with white flowers floating in the water on the table. Finally, she set out the gold-trimmed silverware.

When the table was ready, Emily put a bottle of Champagne on ice and poured cold water into chilled crystal glasses.

Just as she was putting the finishing touches in place, the headlights of a car moved into the driveway and she announced to the crew that the couple had returned.

Excited but secretive, the girls hid in the kitchen while Ana led Reggie to the door.

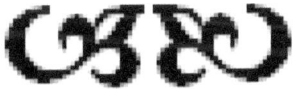

As Ana opened the door to the house, she was surprised at how dark it was. She turned on the foyer light while she led Reggie inside. Then, unaware of the display in the other room, she began to assist Reggie with his things.

"Ana," he said softly.

"Yes, Reggie?"

"Look behind you, dear."

Ana looked at him curiously before she complied with his request. Across the room she could see the flickering lights of candles; surprised, she walked slowly toward the dining room. Reggie hobbled slightly behind her. It was his first peek of the setting and he was pleased.

"What in the world?" she gasped. Her eyes sparkled with wonder. "Mmm, something smells wonderful!"

"The girls outdid themselves, huh?"

"You knew about this?" she asked.

"I did," he confessed.

"This is beautiful," she said. "But are you sure you're up to...?"

"Don't you worry yourself. I'm fine. Tonight is our night. Let's not worry about anything else, okay?"

Ana smiled. "Agreed."

Then, Reggie walked Ana to her chair and pulled it out for her to sit. Then he walked with very little hobbling to his chair. Suddenly, soft music began to play.

Ana smiled whimsically.

Then, Emily entered the room, dressed like a fine waitress. Her growing belly stood out, but she didn't let it get in her way.

"Good evening, folks," she said. "Tonight, at the gentleman's request, we have created your favorites. I hope you enjoy!"

"Oh, my." Ana was smitten through and through.

Emily clapped her hands and Rachel entered, carrying two elegantly decorated plates. Each held a piece of delicious bruschetta. Without saying a word, Rachel placed the dishes in front of the romantic couple and smiled softly. She winked at Reggie and then quietly left the room.

"Ooh, bruschetta!" Ana smiled. She savored every bite.

No sooner had they finished the bruschetta did Amy-Lynn emerge from the kitchen with a beautifully-plated shrimp cocktail. Ana was impressed with how elegant the atmosphere and food was.

The meal continued with the third course of a Caesar salad, then raspberry sorbet, filet mignon, oven-roasted potatoes and baby veggies. The meal wrapped up with a chocolate lava cake, oozing with decadent chocolate warmth.

Ana's senses were pleased.

"What a wonderful dinner," she boasted. "I can't believe you went to all this trouble."

"Well, my dear," Reggie said, "I do have a reason for this."

Ana's eyebrow raised slightly as the kitchen door opened slightly and three sets of spying eyes watched with excitement and hope.

Reggie stood up from the table and Ana was about to rise from her seat. "Stay there, dear," he said as he moved towards the buffet and opened the top drawer. Carefully he removed a tiny box from the drawer and then made his way to Ana's side. Despite the pain in his leg, he knelt down before her and looked her in the eye.

Her big blues began to well up with tears of wonder. *'This isn't happening,'* she thought to herself. *'I'm dreaming.'*

"Ana," he began to speak as tears began to well in his eyes. "Less than a year ago, I thought my life was over, but through grace and a touch of blessed fate, I found you for the second time. Your love, your beauty and your grace have melted my heart and I am, without a doubt, madly in love with you. Although our hearts and hair are full of silver-"

"Speak for yourself, this blonde is all-natural," she snickered. Reggie smiled.

"Okay, well, our hearts are silver, anyhow. And despite our many years of separation and many complications, we found one another again. Now I know what I want in my later years. Ana, it's you. I want you. I love you. You are the reason I wake up each day. You're the reason I can smile. You're the reason I dream. You're the reason I breathe. My bucket list consists of many things: seeing the ocean and visiting exotic places. And now, it includes loving you all my remaining days. Ana, my love, will you do me the honor of becoming my wife? Will you, dear Ana, marry me?"

Ana's lower lip quivered and her hands trembled as Reggie opened the tiny box, revealing the brilliantly bold princess-cut diamond ring. She was so overwhelmed, she could barely find the words to reply.

"Say yes," Amy-Lynn whispered loudly from the door.

"Shhh, Amy-Lynn," Emily scolded.

Ana smiled. With her attention back on Reggie, she nodded her head and said "Yes, Reggie. I will marry you!"

"Yes!" The three young ladies in the kitchen gleefully celebrated.

CHAPTER 34

ANA SOON LEFT her apartment and she and the girls moved to Pennsylvania, happy to be a family again. Reggie's home was full again and a wedding was about to take place. A year had passed since Ruth's death and now spring had come again. The pain had given way to healing and love embraced them all.

Amber stood with Ana proudly as she helped her dress for the wedding. Ana wore a beautiful yellow dress and her girls wore white summer dresses. Cayson was dressed in a tiny tuxedo, while Reggie's grandkids dressed for the part of flower girls.

The backyard had been filled with chairs and it was filling up quickly. Ana looked out the window and smiled. Reggie was nervously fussing with his best men, William and Robert.

Emily and Faith had quickly become great friends, hobbling about with bellies bursting at the seams. Faith left the room and joined the audience while Emily prepared to give her mother away.

"Ready?" Emily asked.

"I'm ready," Ana said. "Girls, you with me?"

"Ready!" Amy-Lynn chimed.

"Definitely ready!" Rachel stated proudly.

With Carl now absent from their life, Reggie had become a role model the girls could look up to and respect. Though it hurt them to be rejected by Carl, they were grateful for Reggie's love; it was real and they embraced it.

As the music began, the girls made their way outside to the awaiting crowd. Reggie's granddaughters and Cayson led the way, sprinkling flower petals on the red runner. The aroma of spring flowers filled the garden. The five-string orchestra played 'Canon in D Major' while Ana followed Amy-Lynn and Rachel to the front of the crowd. Emily waddled proudly on swollen ankles as she led her mom to the front.

Tears of awe flowed from Reggie's eyes as he gazed upon Ana's golden beauty.

"Who gives this woman to be married?"

"I do," Emily said proudly. "Love you, Mom!" She hugged her mother and then took her seat.

"I love you, too." Ana smiled as Emily sat and then turned her attention back to Reggie who stood tall in his dark suit.

"You look beautiful," Reggie whispered.

Ana smiled warmly.

The preacher greeted the guests as he began the ceremony. With long-awaited vows, the high school lovers were joined together as one. With the rings exchanged, the preacher announced them as husband and wife.

A cheer rang through the crowd as tears streamed from the eyes of those who loved them.

The reception was romantic and full of love, laughter, and dancing. As the guests danced, a sudden gasp and cry stopped them cold.

Reggie and Ana spun around to see what had occurred. There, on the dance floor, Faith stood over a large puddle.

"Oh, God!" she cried.

"Oh, God!" William echoed.

Reggie and Ana smiled.

"Sorry, Dad," Faith said apologetically.

"You have nothing to be sorry for. You go. We'll be there soon."

"But your honeymoon..."

"It'll be there when you're done. Don't worry about that."

Reggie and Ana smiled as the wedding ended with the breaking of Faith's water.

"I guess it's time to get this chapter going," Ana suggested.

"I think you may be right."

Reggie and Ana changed into their departure clothes and then made their way to car. As they were walking to the car, Rachel ran outside. "Mom!" she cried.

"Rachel? What is it? You want to come with us?"

"I do, but that's not why I'm worried."

"Mom." Emily walked from the door gripping her belly.

"Are you having contractions?" Ana asked.

"Maybe," she groaned.

"Oh my!" Ana said. "What a night!"

"Let's get you to the hospital dear," Reggie said.

Robert ran from the house when he heard of the newest development. "You two take Emily to the hospital. I'll bring Amy-Lynn and Rachel as soon as I get Nora and the baby home."

"Thanks, Robert," Ana said as she loaded her daughter into the car.

CHAPTER 35

ANA WAS with Emily during her delivery while everyone else waited anxiously in the waiting room. William and Faith were a few doors down preparing for their delivery.

"You can do it!" William cheered.

Faith groaned and cried in agony as she pushed out the emerging child.

"One more, good one," the doctor announced.

Faith gave it her all and with one big push, a new life came slipping out into the doctor's waiting hands. William's eyes were full of tears as he beheld his beautiful baby boy.

Meanwhile, down the hall, Emily was about to deliver her second child. Her labor had moved along quickly, and with a few pushes and all her mother's support, the crown of her child's head could be seen. With one last push, Emily's child was free.

"It's a girl!" Ana cried.

Emily's eyes streamed with joy as the doctor laid the mess-covered baby in her arms.

Ana and William emerged from their rooms almost simultaneously.

"Well?" Ana asked.

"It's a boy!" William cried.

"Congratulations!" Ana said giving him a celebratory hug.

"And yours?"

"A girl!" Ana gleamed.

"Congratulations to you, too!"

Ana and William exited the delivery area and announced their joy together. The wonder was overwhelming.

"What a wedding day, huh?" Amy-Lynn asked.

"One for the record books!" Reggie confessed.

"And I wouldn't have changed a thing," Ana added.

"Me either," Reggie agreed.

CS 80

Once the women were moved into their room, the families joined to meet their newest additions.

"He's gorgeous," Ana said.

"William and I wanted to ask you something," Faith said.

"Sure," Ana replied. "Anything."

"We'd like... if it's okay... to name our son after David. Would that be alright?"

Ana's jaw dropped, along with Amy-Lynn and

Rachel's. Ana began to sob. "Yes. I would love that," she said. "Thank you so much!"

"I also have a question," Emily said, holding her daughter in the opposite bed.

"Yes, dear?" Ana replied.

"Not for you, Mom. For Reggie."

"Yes, Emily?" he replied.

"I'd love to name my daughter Ruth, after your late wife. I know she was an amazing woman to have had a man as wonderful as you," she said.

Reggie was honored. "I would like that." Then with a hug and a kiss, Reggie hugged Emily and the tiny Ruth she held.

With a day and a half of amazing love and celebration, Reggie and Ana finally made their way to their awaiting ship and sailed out into the big blue Pacific. With the joy of love behind them, with them, and before them, they embraced one another, enjoying the wonders of breaching whales and celebrating the second chance they'd both been given.

"This will be hard to top," Ana admitted.

"Maybe," Reggie admitted. "But I sure as hell am going to enjoy trying."

"Me, too. Me, too!"

As the sun set over the giant blue whales, the couple sealed their hearts of silver with a kiss an eternal vow of love.

ABOUT THE AUTHOR

Emilie Hamdan is an emerging erotica author of many erotica kinks and sub-genres. Be sure to check out other books and leave a review if this story got you hot!

Visit my blog at Emilie Hamdan Blog

Join my newsletter for the exclusive Emilie Hamdan Newsletter

Sign up for Free Stories from Xplicit Press Authors

Xplicit Press Author Updates

Like Xplicit Press on Facebook

Follow Xplicit Press on Twitter

Readers: I want to expand a few of the stories to see where the characters can be explored further. If there are any of the stories that you would like to read more about again, I'd love to hear from you!

Keep In Touch
Emilie Hamdan
info@emiliehamdan.com